THE AMAZ
SEL

"In *The Amazing Adventures of Selma Calderón* I stepped into a magical world where I could feel the characters' emotions. Excited, nervous, and always wanting to know what would happen next, I did not want to put this book down."

—Diego Esparza, 7th grade

"Rebecca Villarreal's middle school novel uses magic realism to capture the attention of young readers while introducing people and places of note—from the poet Lucille Clifton to the Alhambra in Spain. Every child who has wished they could use magic to travel (and who hasn't?) will enjoy seeing the world with Selma Calderón, especially when she skips class to travel to do research for a school assignment. *The Amazing Adventures of Selma Calderón* taps all the senses with aromas and tastes of chilaquiles in Chicago and chocolate croissants in Paris, the light and colors of the Alhambra, and the sounds of poetry at home. In an age-appropriate way, the reader also sees Selma deal with a range of emotions, from happiness with her friend Hurley to grief at the loss (possibly abandonment) of her parents."

—Deborah Menkart, Executive Director,
Teaching for Change

THE AMAZING ADVENTURES

OF

SELMA CALDERÓN

THE AMAZING ADVENTURES
OF
SELMA CALDERÓN

A Globetrotting Magical Mystery

of

Courage, Food & Friendship

Book 1
Truth & Magic Series

REBECCA VILLARREAL

MAMA
CHELO
PRESS

CARPINTERIA, CALIFORNIA

Credit: Lucille Clifton, "atlas" from The Book of Light. Copyright © 1993 by Lucille Clifton. Reprinted with the permission of The Permissions Company, Inc. on behalf of Copper Canyon Press, www.coppercanyonpress.org.

Published by Mama Chelo Press
1072 Casitas Pass Road, #180, Carpinteria, CA 93013
Place special or bulk orders via mamachelopress@gmail.com
Get our Tribe & Family Book Club Guide and more:
www.rebeccavillarreal.com

Cover design by Bookish Design
Book design by Stacey Aaronson

Library of Congress Control Number: 2015908278
ISBN (print): 978-0-9962088-2-6
ISBN (e-book): 978-0-9962088-1-9

Printed in the U.S.A.
First Print Edition: 2015
First E-Book Edition: 2015

Dedicated to my husband, José,
my son, Jacob,
and my dear one, Victor

You live in my heart, and you don't even pay rent.

Vives en mi corazón, y ni siquiera pagas renta.

—Mama Chelo

Table of Contents

1

Cucalacas

Selma

TRAVELING BY MAGIC can be a little risky, but it's also exciting! Just a few more days and I'm headed to Paris during school. It'll be my first time using magic to go from one country to another. I'll miss Mrs. Cushing's technology class, but I'll definitely be back in time for Mr. Aguirre's music class.

Now that I'm in fifth grade, I think I'm ready to test my powers more. Guadey started teaching me spells when I turned eight. Guadey's my guardian. She and my mom were best friends since elementary school. She's been taking care of me since I was two.

I have so many wishes. I want to know more about magic. I want to learn more about my parents. Guadey told me they were in a boating accident. That was so long ago now, I can't remember them. And whenever I ask questions, she gives me short answers. Like when I asked how they met, she said, "They met in the Atlantic Ocean and fell in love." She won't give me any details. When I asked her about my last name, she said it comes from my mom's side, which seems weird. Why wouldn't I have my dad's last name? Anyhow, she said my mom was part Mexican and part Polish. I think if I can get better at spells, I can use magic to remember how we used to play, what both my parents looked like, and even what they smelled like.

Part of the reason I want to use magic to travel is because I've always dreamed of exploring the world by eating all the foods that are special in each country. I've been having fun at home pretending I live in another place, cooking new foods, and then eating them. But now, I want to do it for real.

Someday, I'll own the coolest restaurant filled with my favorite dishes from all my adventures around the world. After people eat their meals, I'll blast some music and we'll push back the chairs and tables and dance every single night.

I actually started learning spells just by watching Guadey, and then I begged her to teach me. I experimented with our cat, Uli, whose full name is Ulises. I could tell he didn't really like it the time I turned him into a dog. Guadey didn't really like it either. She explained that the world isn't ready for magic in an open way. Some people are afraid of it, and some people might try to use it—or use *us*—to do bad things. So I keep it a secret.

Guadey stores a wooden recipe box filled with spells on top of the fridge. I remember the first time I learned how to do a transportation spell from Guadey. When she walked into my room, I was sitting at my desk writing a menu for my restaurant with red, purple, and green markers.

"Hi, Selma," she said, peeking over my shoulder. "I like your choice of colors."

"Thanks!" I said, looking up. That's when I noticed she was holding her recipe box. "What are you doing with that?"

"I'm going to teach you a transportation spell."

I jumped out of my chair and clapped my hands quickly over and over. "Really? You're actually going to teach me a spell I can do all by myself?"

"Yes," Guadey said, "that's exactly what we're going to do."

Guadey was wearing a long, flowing, bright pink skirt. She sat down right in the middle of my room so her skirt spread out around her like a big flower.

"Wow! Let's do it!" I hopped from where I was standing and plopped down so I was facing her, sitting cross-legged. She placed the box on top of her skirt and pulled out a card. I leaned forward to look inside the box, but she quickly snapped it shut.

"This is a basic transportation spell, Selma. For now, it can be used to move from room to room in our apartment. When your magic is stronger, you can create your own unique spells to travel longer distances, even between countries."

My eyes opened wide and I showed my toothiest smile.

"But for now," she said, "it's important to never try this spell without letting me know."

I nodded. I was already breathing fast. I felt like I was about to ride a roller coaster, and I couldn't help but think how cool it would be to travel the world once I mastered the spell. "I understand. Can we please get started? I can't wait!"

"Yes, but before we do, there's one word missing from the spell. It's your magical word. Everyone has their own unique word, and I selected yours for you."

My mouth dropped open but nothing came out.

"I can see you're excited." Guadey laughed a little, took my hand, and leaned over to me. She whispered in my ear, "It's *Cucalacas*."

"Oooh, I like the way that sounds," I said.

Guadey leaned back and watched me. "Go

ahead and say it, Selma. You need to feel comfortable with the word rolling around in your mouth."

I put my hands palms up on my knees like I've seen people do when they meditate, closed my eyes, and said, "Cu ... ca ... la ... cas!"

Guadey smiled. "Say it again, three times in a row."

"Cucalacas! Cucalacas! Cucalacas!"

My stomach jumped in a fun way. It felt like I was on the Tilt-A-Whirl ride at a carnival.

"Great job, honey," Guadey said. "I think you're ready to learn more about the spell."

My eyes got really big.

"The plan is for you to move from your room to the kitchen. But before you recite the spell, you need to think of a specific spot in the kitchen and imagine how you will physically end up."

I nodded, starting to picture myself there.

"Now, since you're doing this spell while sitting, you should keep it simple and picture yourself landing on the floor of the kitchen right next to the refrigerator door, sitting just like you are now. Envision that spot and see yourself there. That's the only thing you can keep in your mind, okay?"

"Okay," I said, closing my eyes. But I was so excited, I started thinking about all the places in the world I could go and didn't see the kitchen.

"Focus, Selma. Think about the kitchen," Guadey said.

My eyes popped open. "How'd you know ...?"

"I know you," Guadey smiled. "Now, close your eyes again. What does the floor look like? How close will you be sitting to the fridge? Will you be facing the fridge or facing the kitchen table?"

I closed my eyes, took a deep breath in, then let it out slowly. I thought about the ocean blue tiles on the floor. I saw the fridge full of my drawings and magnets. "I'm ready to read it now, Guadey."

She handed me the card and I said the words out loud.

Hallow there
Hallow here
Walls melt now
There's no fear
Bring me to another place
Bright new vision for my face
Cucalacas!

The next thing I knew, I was in the kitchen sitting cross-legged, looking at my drawing of the Eiffel Tower in Paris stuck to the fridge by our Phillies magnet. My belly felt a bit woozy like I just went down a big slope on a roller coaster. I stood up a little too quickly and had to grab the fridge handle for balance. Then I started yelling as I ran back to my room.

"I did it, Guadey! I did it! It was just like you said!"

Guadey was still sitting in the same position with a big grin on her face. "Great job, Selma! I'm so happy for you. Your very first lesson worked perfectly. Now, have a seat so I can tell you a bit more about what it means to have powers."

I started to sit down but caught a glimpse of my hair in the mirror. It looked like I just took a ride in a convertible. I started to giggle but then saw Guadey's face had gone serious. That was when she began to explain the rules of magic. Like how I'm not allowed to do spells on people unless I'm afraid they're going to hurt me or someone else. Also, I'm never allowed to perform spells at school. There's too much risk of people finding out. She also explained her own powers. Guadey has an extra strong connection to me like a mother would have with a daughter. Even if she isn't my real mom, I love her like one. She says that because of our love and our powers, she can tune into me like when you pick a channel on TV. If she tunes into my channel, she can sense what I'm doing or if I'm in trouble.

"That's why I'll know if you try using magic for short cuts, like putting your dishes in the sink after meals or for doing homework," she said. "Magic is a precious resource and we don't want to waste it on silly things we can do ourselves." She also said it's important that I learn to be responsible and do what other kids do, which is why I still have to make my bed and take out the garbage. At least I earn an allowance. I'm up to $3.00 a week, and Guadey says when I take on more chores, I'll earn $5.00.

We moved to Chicago in July. Our new apartment is in a neighborhood called Pilsen just eight blocks from my school. The whole place feels magical. There was an artist who lived here before us, so the ceiling in my room has its very own painting. When I lie in bed, I look up at a beautiful woman with skin like *cajeta* (that's an awesome Mexican caramel made with goat's milk) and long, thick, brown hair ending in swirls. She kind of reminds me of Guadey. And there's a man who's singing while playing a guitar. The sky all around them is light blue with clouds, but it's not a normal sky. There are individual ribbons of green, red, yellow, and a deep, deep purple floating and twisting through the whole painting. One of my favorite parts is where the artist wrote in flowing black letters: "*música, canto y pensamiento*." Music, singing, and thought!

The whole apartment is like a long freight train with room after room. Just inside the door, the living room is on the left, followed by the dining room. My room is next to Guadey's bedroom across from the dining room on the right. A little farther down is the bathroom, and then the kitchen is at the very end with Guadey's study off it, kind of tucked away in its own corner.

One of the first things Guadey did after we moved in was put the wooden recipe box on top of the fridge. She told me it was locked with a spell. "Let me be clear, Selma," she said, "there's a magical alarm set on this box. You'll get caught and there will be consequences if you ever try to open it. It's out here in plain sight to remind you to have patience and practice. The better you do with the spells I've already taught you, the more likely I can teach you more."

It's now the second week in September and the beginning of the third week of school. When we first moved here, Guadey taught me a new spell every couple of days. But since school started, she hasn't taught me any new ones. This morning I'm lying in bed extra long, thinking about and planning my trip to Paris. I've also been practicing my French. *Bonjour. Ça va? Ça va bien, et toi?* If I can basically say hello, how are you, and point at the food I want, I should be okay. After all, I'm almost ten and a half years old.

I think I've learned enough to take my first trip alone, and I've been working on a spell to get there. I already know I'll need to wear warm clothes because it's kind of cold and rainy there right now. But that's okay because I plan to duck into a warm café for a hot buttery croissant with chocolate inside and a *café au lait*. A lot of people think fifth grade is too young for coffee, but Guadey and I don't think so. I see kids at school with Coke, Gatorade, Doritos, and Gummy Worms, all of which have no major nutritional value and are full of chemicals.

Coffee, especially café au lait, is a source of calcium and helps me stay awake for Mr. Finncrisp's class. He teaches geography and social studies, but he's never actually been anywhere. So when he talks about people, places, and foods, it's flat—all on paper. He sometimes gets mad at me because I ask him a lot of detailed questions he can't answer about places that aren't in the book. And he refuses to look it up on the Internet because he says he learned from books, and if it was good enough for him, then it's good enough for us. He gets me so frustrated. Sometimes I think if he had the power to erase my curiosity the way he erases the board, he would do just that. I better hurry up and finish getting ready. It's past time to leave for school. I'm so excited we have art class today.

I can't believe school's out already and I'm on my way home. Today the sky is the color of wet, gray slate. I'm excited because the city is getting geared up for the Chicago Marathon. Guadey says I should start training with my friend Hurley so we can run a few blocks of the race from Ashland Avenue all the way to Halsted Street. Hurley moved to Chicago at the same time I moved here, only he moved from North Carolina instead of Philadelphia. He's my first real friend here. Even though this is only my third week at school, I feel like I can trust him. Maybe someday I can even tell him about my powers.

I wonder if anyone noticed that I did a spell to make art class last longer because we were making those gods' eyes out of popsicle sticks and yarn, and I hadn't finished mine yet. I also changed the water in the drinking fountain to iced tea. It left the principal, Mrs. Catania, totally confused. I know Guadey said not to do magic at school, but the kids liked it, so we had plenty of energy all day.

But not everything I do at school involves magic. I like to do lots of helpful things, like clean the board and help Hurley with his math homework. I also like to help Mrs. Cushing make sure all the computers are logged out at the end of our class.

I'm super hungry for dinner already, even though it's still the afternoon and not dinnertime yet. Last night Guadey made my favorite, *chilaquiles*. She blended stewed tomatoes and chipotle peppers, then mixed them with tortilla chips, onions, and scrambled eggs. We added avocado and *queso fresco* on top. It's one of my favorite mouth experiences because there's a slight crunch from the chips and then my tongue gets a tingle from the chipotle, and the sautéed onions actually turn a little sweet. The scrambled egg is like the goodness glue that sticks it all together. I can't wait to heat up the leftovers when I get home.

2

Guardian

Guadey

EVERYONE CALLS ME GUADEY—that's short for Guadalupe. I always say Selma was born into a family of three: her mother, her father, and me. After a lifetime in Philly, I was awarded a fellowship to teach poetry at the University of Illinois at Chicago. Now we live in this city mapped by the cobalt blues of Lake Michigan and the steely elevated trains snaking through neighborhoods, bursting with foods from every corner of the planet. Selma already loves it here.

She's planning a trip to France followed by some quiet time on the San Juan Islands. I know this because she tells me her plans ... most of the time. I expect she'll continue to add more places to her wish list.

I enrolled her in school at Kahlo Community Academy, a public school where the students have to wear uniforms—which makes my life easier because getting dressed for school is simple. I only wish the rest of our life could be that easy. I have a feeling Selma's thirst for knowledge about our magical heritage could bring back some vengeful ghosts from my past. I use magic to tune into her as much as I can to anticipate any spells she might try. It's not easy keeping up with her. She needs careful instruction, but her nature is to absorb lessons everywhere she goes.

I remember learning how to say a spell in my head for the first time. Soleymani taught me in college. He was a fellow student who took me to the sea. He won my heart. That feels so long ago. I wish he were here to help me with Selma. I wish her parents were here too.

3

To Paris

Selma

IT'S FRIDAY AND THE END of my third week of school. I was such a slowpoke this morning that Guadey decided to use magic to get me to school on time. With her help, I made it to homeroom a little early, so I'm waiting for Hurley. I'm glad to be inside because it's cold here for September! I have to put on tights under my pants every day.

Even though I just started school, I'm feeling like I could use a vacation because moving from Philly and getting used to a new city and a new school is a little tiring. Guadey says if I do my homework for real and don't use magic, then I can go to Paris for vacation over Christmas.

But what if I have to go to Paris to *do* my homework? I mean, Mr. Finncrisp did assign us a city profile for a project. Why should I spend time inside a book when I could do the real thing? In fact, I've been practicing enough that I think I'm ready to travel to Paris *today*. My magic feels stronger than ever. If all goes as planned, I can be back in time for Mr. Aguirre's music class. Oh! There's Hurley in the hallway, right next to our lockers. We were so lucky to get lockers next to each other. I'll ask him to cover for me.

"Hey, Hurley."

"Hey, Selma. What's goin' on?"

Hurley has a really noticeable Southern accent, so some of the kids at school make fun of him. I wish they'd just leave him alone.

"I need to get some research done for Mr. Finn-crisp's class, so I'm going to be gone this afternoon starting at lunch. Can you cover for me? Say you think I went home sick?"

"Sure ... but you're not going to get in any trouble, are you?"

"Naaah, don't worry about me. I'll be back before you know it."

It took forever for lunchtime to arrive. When Hurley and I leave math class, he turns left to go downstairs to the cafeteria, and I walk down the hallway to the girls' bathroom. I know it will be empty because everyone heads downstairs for lunch. I feel kind of bad leaving Hurley alone since we usually sit together, but I can't wait any longer for my trip. I only have about 90 minutes including lunch and technology class with Mrs. Cushing. Hurley will make excuses for me with Mrs. Cushing, but I just don't want to miss Mr. Aguirre's music class. I have a feeling he would ask too many questions and I don't want to get Hurley in trouble.

I step into the bathroom stall that's farthest away from the door. Then I stick my Moleskine notebook, felt-tip pen, and camera inside my jacket pockets so they don't get left behind. I recite the spell:

Cross my arms, cross my feet,
Cross my fingers and my toes,
Paris, Paris, come to me.
Eiffel Tower, Notre Dame,
At your sight, I'll never be the same!
Cucalacas!

I made it! I'm a little dizzy, and I have to figure out where I am exactly. Okay, there's the Seine River ... turn around ... hoorah! There's Notre Dame! It's so big! There are tons of carvings and windows and points and spires. It's going to be hard not to run over there. I'm taking a few quick pictures of it, but I have to stay focused on my research. I'm at *la rue St-Julien-le-Pauvre*, in the Latin Quarter, also known as the 5th *arrondissement*. *Arrondissements* are kind of like neighborhoods. I'm just a block and a half from that bakery I read about in the *Lonely Planet* guidebook I borrowed from Mr. Finncrisp's classroom. Gosh, I'm glad I'm wearing tights here too. It's drizzly and chilly, but not quite as cold as Chicago. The rain brings out the wet grass smell of the river, plus the damp pavement reminds me of the smell of clay. And it's so beautiful!

I just need to walk a little bit. I stop to look at the iron railings on the windows, and how every building and café looks different. There are shutters on some windows, and some have yellow and red flowers hanging out of wooden boxes. And wow! There's a restaurant called *La Surprise*. I thought it was a flower store because there are green leaves all around the sign and the biggest philodendron I've ever seen, along with bushy pink and lavender flowers. I wish I could share this moment with Guadey. I feel like I'm walking through a pretty postcard.

Here I am at *la rue Lagrange*. I love the way this *boulangerie* takes up the whole corner. This one doesn't have outdoor seating like lots of cafés I've read about. Instead, there's a wall of floor-to-ceiling windows that make up a sort of outdoor enclosed porch, perfect for a drizzly day like today. A green awning with white words wraps around the entire corner. It says: "*Boulanger*," "*Salon de Thé*," "*Glacier*," "*Patissier*," and "*Chocolatier*." That means they have bread, tea, ice cream, and most importantly, pastries and chocolate! I'm sure they also sell coffee.

Let's see ... oh, I need money. In 2002, they changed the money from francs to euros. But I wish I could still use francs. They looked so cool—each one had the picture of someone famous with just their head kind of big taking up about half of one side. Each bill had detailed scenes using every color imaginable. The 10,000 franc note showed a picture of the Arc de Triomphe. It's a giant arch built to honor the soldiers who fought for France in wars through the centuries. I learned that the Arc is the center of what they call *L'Axe Historique*, like a vortex for all the major roads and important sites in Paris. There's got to be a cool mystery to uncover there.

Now, to get some money from the ATM. Lucky I brought my magic ATM card. Guadey says I can use it anywhere in the world, but mostly for emergencies —and truly, this is sort of a homework emergency.

I'm not sure of the French word for withdrawal, but I'll try pushing buttons. Excellent! I guessed right. The word is *retrait*. Now I'm off to purchase my research—an authentic French *pain au chocolat!*

The café windows have this sort of golden glow from the frosty glass light shades hanging from the ceiling. I can see my reflection in the window. My bangs are sticking straight up from the trip, which reminds me of the time Guadey taught me my first transportation spell. I pull my hair back in a pony-tail. I can flatten my bangs once I get in there. For now, I'm mesmerized by all the pastries. I think I see Napoleons layered with flaky crust and whipped cream ... and almond croissants ... and there's my favorite, *pain au chocolate!*

Here goes. I grab hold of the small brass door handle and oh my, I feel like I'm under a spell as I walk in. The sneaky scent of espresso and smells of dark chocolate, powdered sugar, and fresh butter are tickling my nose. There's a perfect table in the back, and luckily only one person is there. I'm hoping he'll finish his cigarette soon and go. That's another thing I read about the French: many people love their cigarettes. Yuck!

The man behind the counter has flour on his shirt and a mustache that looks like he painted it on with a black marker. He gives me a big smile and nods. I'm going to do my best with my French.

"*Bonjour! Un pain au chocolat avec café au lait, s'il vous plaît.*"

"*Oui, mademoiselle,*" he says.

The smoking guy gets up to leave so I grab his seat before someone else can. I hope the smoke smell goes away before my order comes. A few minutes later, the man with the mustache brings me a pretty cup and my pastry on a small plate with pink vines and leaves all around the rim. It smells like pastries again in here, so I lean over and inhale the buttery smell of the crusty layers and that block of dark chocolate melted inside. I poke my finger right in the middle just to see the crust bounce back slowly.

Now for my first bite. Oh my goodness. The flaky layers from the top are filled with air, and the buttery bottom layers are solid, but the best part is the way the chocolate surprises my mouth at every other bite. It's not overwhelmingly chocolate; it just makes your taste buds want to search for the chocolate in the bite. I could sing out loud, it's so delicious! My fingers are already so shiny just from touching the *pain au chocolat* that I can almost see my reflection in my palm. Now I can flatten my bangs with my fingers since they're all buttery—it's kind of like hair gel. (Good thing I have brown hair—I don't think you can really tell that I used butter.) And the *café au lait* is creamy and strong. Oh, how happy I am just sitting here by myself sipping this frothy wonder!

Here comes a family. This little French kid can barely see into the glass case filled with pastries, but he seems like he knows what he wants because he's pointing right at the Napoleon. I bet you he'll have whipped cream all over his face in a matter of minutes. Boy, do the French know how to slow down and enjoy life.

I wish I could slow down, but this is so delicious that I can't stop devouring it. I'm already licking the last crumbs and chocolate smears off my fingers and sipping my last drops. I don't have much time, so I need to figure out where to go next. I bring my dirty dishes to the counter and head out.

The cold hits my face as I open the door, but I still want to take a little walk along the river. Oh look, there's the *Bateaux Mouche*! That's the tourist boat. I've made it to the bridge, and everyone is taking pictures as they go by. I'm going to pretend I'm French and welcome them to Paris. "*Bienvenue à Paris!*" I yell, waving at them as they take pictures of me. I bet they think I'm French.

I come back from the bridge and walk along the damp sidewalk. On this trip, I'm not focusing on the big tourist sites like the Eiffel Tower or the Notre Dame cathedral, even though it's tempting. I just want to walk around like I live here. I think this is the best way to get to know a city and its people—at least that's the way I've been exploring Pilsen.

As I walk around, it's starting to clear up a bit. The setting sun is poking through the clouds, and the drizzle has changed into a gentle sun shower. I have my dark green raincoat, and I like the rain. On the *Quai*—or the riverside sidewalk—alongside the Seine, there's a row of newsstands with a bunch of old books and magazines, but I'm mostly interested in the old postcards. I buy one with a panoramic view of Paris and the Arc de Triomphe. It's so old. At first I thought it was a photograph, but when I look more closely, I can see that someone drew a picture of the river and the arch. They did such a good job with all the details, even the individual carvings. The neat thing is that it was sent to Barcelona in 1917 on January 10—wow! That was a long time ago! The postcard is written in Spanish, and I know Spanish better than I know French, so let's see if I can translate:

Dear Marsé,

I received with much happiness your two postcards, and I did not answer because I waited until I found this one at the end of December. I wish you all the best in the New Year and the same for your family.

I suppose you have visited all your old friends in that nice city.

Until soon dear friend,
(Signature that I can't read)

P.S. Always remember the Alhambra.

It's fun to think about things that happened a long time ago. I wonder what this person meant by "remember the Alhambra." I'm pretty sure that's in Spain. I'm going to write that down in my notebook for future research.

I check my watch, which is still on Chicago time. I've been here for almost an hour and a half, and I have to get back in time for Mr. Aguirre's class. I quickly buy a map of the Paris metro system to use in my report, then duck behind a kiosk where no one will see me disappear when I say my spell.

Cross my arms, cross my feet,
Cross my toes and my fingers,
Take me where my grade school lingers!
Cucalacas!

I made it! I'm in the janitor's closet. I can still taste the flaky crust and chocolate, and the bitter coffee flavor is sitting at the back of my tongue, balancing out the sweet of the *pain au chocolat.* I'll open the closet door when the halls are clear and everyone's in class. I don't want anyone to see me come out of here.

When it's quiet, I walk down the hall to Mr. Aguirre's classroom. I slip into the back and slide a pencil across the floor to get Hurley's attention so he doesn't worry, but it doesn't matter now because Mr. Aguirre's looking right at me. Here it comes.

"So, Ms. Calderón."

Mr. Aguirre always says my name with a super Mexican accent, but then switches back to his Chicago accent, which is so different from how we talk in Philly. It's like his mouth closes up words so that "Thanks" sounds like "Thenks." He also says "washroom" instead of bathroom or restroom.

"Tell me what brings you to my class late and not in your assigned seat."

I know Mr. Aguirre isn't really mad. He's always nice to me. He just laughs when I tell him the truth (which he thinks I'm just making up).

"I was doing research for my homework for Mr. Finncrisp's class."

"Oh, what kind of research were you doing that makes you late for class?"

"I went to Paris to try a real chocolate croissant and *café au lait* and to walk along the Seine River."

Hurley turns around and raises his eyebrows at me. But Mr. Aguirre just laughs and says, "Well, Ms. Calderón, next time, catch an earlier flight back."

"Sure thing, Mr. Aguirre."

When music class is over, Hurley comes running up to me.

"Dang, Selma. What took you so long?"

"What do you mean? Like I said, I went to Paris to do research for Mr. Finncrisp's class."

"Yeah, right. Like you could really go to Paris."

I look down at the toes of my black school shoes. I wish I could tell Hurley the truth. But I feel a lump in my throat because I've never told anyone about my magic, and even if Hurley were the first, what if he's scared or doesn't trust me or doesn't want to be my friend? I put my hands together like I'm going to say a prayer, take a deep breath, and blow out the air. "Can I trust you, Hurley?"

"Of course, Selma."

"Okay, the thing is ... I have magic powers. I can do spells and things ... I'm still learning, though. "

Hurley looks at me a while longer. Finally, a giant grin spreads across his face. "I've known all along you had something going on."

"Yeah?" I say, arching my left eyebrow and wondering if Hurley has really been on to me.

"I remember when we had iced tea in the water fountains. The first day of school, you told me your list of favorite things and iced tea was number four. It's no big deal ... I'm around that stuff all the time. My mom reads tea leaves. She just prays over them before she shares her predictions."

The lump in my throat gets smaller until it disappears. I stand there with an open-mouthed smile. I didn't know Hurley believed in magic. I'm so excited that I lean toward him and put my hands on his shoulders and my face right in front of his. "Well, Hurley, maybe now you can come on my next trip with me!"

"Where are you going?"

"I'm planning to go to East Africa. A little Kenya, a little Tanzania, and then we'll go to Uganda and visit Bwindi Impenetrable National Forest to see the mountain gorillas!"

"Wow! Sounds like fun. We're going to need to come up with a story for my mom, though."

"Okay, we'll think about it a little more. Let's go to the library."

"Yeah, let's check out some books, then let's play marbles back in Mr. Aguirre's room before his next class starts. His room is free this period."

I smile because I know I can count on Hurley for one thing: he always wants to play marbles.

4

Hail

Hurley

I'VE BEEN AT KAHLO Community Academy for three weeks now. I'm so glad it's Friday afternoon and I can just sit on my kitchen floor and play marbles. Mom let me paint a circle here so I can play even when the weather is bad.

My name, Hurley, comes from a distant uncle, who everybody says has a lot of Lumbee tribe blood in him. I have two middle names, Nathaniel and Bartholomew. I think my mom just liked both names and couldn't decide. My dad's name is Wendell Bingenworth. He gave me my first bag of marbles. He moved away when I was six, and I haven't heard from him in a really long time.

I met Selma on the first day of school. There aren't a lot of black kids there; most of the students are Mexican, even if they were born here. And nobody comes from North Carolina, so nobody talks like I do. Right away the kids started picking on me. When they do that, I just put my special marbles in my pocket and keep rubbing them together. The one who picks on me the most is Xavier Serrano. Everybody calls him "X." He walks around Kahlo like a big, puffed-up rooster. His dad owns the Serrano *Carnicería*, which is the biggest butcher shop in Pilsen. He eats meat for breakfast, lunch, and dinner.

On my first day when Mrs. Catania was introducing me to the class, X started in on me when I said I'd never seen hail before (we had a freak hailstorm right before school started). After class, X started talking really slowly and calling me "Hail Baby," which makes no sense. He's not that smart. He's just big and eats a lot of meat.

Just then, Selma walked up. She's not afraid of X. I found that out real fast.

"X, I smell a meat fart. Did you make a meat fart?" asked Selma.

"Shut up, Selma," X said, smirking at me.

But Selma wouldn't stop. "For real, X, what did you eat for breakfast? Was it pork or beef? Because I keep two different air fresheners in my locker. Lavender sometimes covers up your pork farts, but only evergreen-scented disinfectant can kill those beef farts."

Honestly, I don't think X had farted at all at that point. But Selma talking about it so much even made my stomach start to rumble.

All of a sudden, X let a big one rip with all his friends standing behind him. They couldn't keep straight faces because it smelled so bad. X tried to pass it off like his sneaker scuffed the floor and made the fart noise.

Selma said, "Uh-oh, it looks like this calls for evergreen. Come on, Hurley. The noses of Kahlo Community Academy are counting on us."

And from then on, we've been friends.

Back home I had some friends, but they were jealous because I was the marble champion at school. I kept all my marbles lined up in my room in mayonnaise jars. But soon I kept beating so many people that nobody had any marbles left to play with me. So I figured when I came to Chicago, I'd keep a low profile with my marbles. And it's a good thing I did, because I bet you X would try to steal them.

Mom didn't want to move my marbles all the way to Chicago from Charlotte, but I begged and begged her. Sometimes my thumb gets sore from hitting them, so I use a Band-Aid for extra padding and that seems to work. I usually play a game called "ringer." Gosh, I would have loved to be in the first-ever national marbles tournament in 1922. It's still held every year. I'm hoping to enter it when I'm twelve. That's why I practice every day.

Some kids just sit in front of the TV and play video games. Not me. There's always more to learn about marbles. They used to be made with clay and were called "common marbles." Then there were crockery marbles, or "crockies." The kinds of glass marbles are endless, and the agates are hardest to find. Sometimes I just line up my favorites along the windowsill and imagine they're planets with their own worlds going on inside.

My mom, Hildegarde, has always wanted to live in Chicago with the skyscrapers and all the musical history. She likes blues a lot—jazz, too—but she really prefers the blues. It's not like she couldn't find blues in the South, but I guess there's something about the music scene here. She did a lot of research from Charlotte and found herself a good job at *The Chicago Tribune*, doing layout and design. Back in Charlotte, she worked for a company that made most of the high school yearbooks for schools all over the country. She started in the mailroom and then learned the graphic design computer programs so she could help design the yearbooks. That's what got her a job up here.

She picked Pilsen as our neighborhood because it's close to downtown and still affordable. We live on Laflin Street in a three-bedroom row house. I didn't mind leaving Charlotte because about a year before we moved, Mom started bringing me all these library books on Chicago, and it seemed (except for the cold) like it would be more exciting than North Carolina.

I certainly didn't expect to meet my best friend here and that she would have magical powers.

5

Busted

Selma

IT'S MONDAY MORNING AND my fourth week of school. I'm so excited to give my Paris report today. I meet Guadey in the kitchen.

"Good morning, Guadey!"

"Good morning, Selma. You're dressed early this morning. Are you ready to make chocolate croissants for your school report?"

"Yes! Oh, and before I forget, is it okay for Hurley to come over after school tomorrow since you're not teaching any afternoon classes?"

"Sure. Let me know if you want me to make anything spe—"

"*Chilaquiles!*" I blurt out. "But please don't make them too spicy because Hurley told me he doesn't like spicy food. And also, would you please pick up an *empanada de camote* for him? I think he'll be surprised by how it tastes like a sweet potato pie in a pocket!"

"Sure, honey. I'll do that. But I want you to be on time for school, so let's get started making the croissants. I'll walk you there and help you carry everything. And I'm giving you permission this one time to use magic in school to heat the croissants right before you give your report. You can do the spell in your head without saying it out loud, just the way I taught you."

I nod and smile as Guadey says, "Go pull together the ingredients. I'll get the tray. Oh! And I bought you these," she says, waving a pack of napkins with Eiffel Towers on them.

"Wow! Thanks, Guadey."

I grab the crescent rolls. We use the ones in a tube from Immaculate Baking Company. Here's how we do it:

First, I peel the wrapper from around the tube— but I always keep it nearby because the directions are written on it. Guadey shows me how to preheat the oven to 350 degrees. Then, I hold the tube tightly, poke a spoon into the seam, and poof! It opens. Now I carefully separate the triangles of dough. It's important to place a small amount of chocolate chips, about eight to ten, on the widest corner of each triangle. Then I roll that corner closed and keep rolling it until I have a snake with a fat, chocolate middle. After that, I place it on the baking sheet and turn the corners in toward each other so that it's shaped like a crescent moon. I bake them for ten to fifteen minutes until they are golden. The kids at school are going to love these!

"Ms. Calderón, you're up next."

I come to the front of the classroom. "Thanks, Mr. Finncrisp. Hi, everyone. I'd like to start my presentation with some food. Here, Mr. Finncrisp, you can have the first hot chocolate croissant." I hand him an extra shiny buttery one that's got chocolate oozing out of one side.

Somebody in the back of class yells out, "Pass some back here!"

"They're coming!" I say. "Let me officially start my report." I take a deep breath and begin.

"Paris is a city of many wonders and lots of interesting history. But it's also a place of delicious food. This is a chocolate croissant—" I hold one up. "Or sometimes they call it *pain au chocolat* when it's in a different shape. It means bread with chocolate." I turn to Hurley with the tray of croissants and the napkins. "Hurley, will you please pass these out while I share some more facts about Paris?"

Hurley walks around the classroom and hands one croissant to each student. Clare O'Connor jumps up to help even though I didn't ask her. She grabs the napkins from Hurley and walks behind him, handing one to each student. She stands out with her bright green eyes and her green dress. She loves green. Sometimes I think she likes Hurley.

I continue my presentation. "Paris is the capital of France. There are more than two million people living there. It's the most popular place for tourists in the whole world. More than 30 million people go there every year. The city is located on the Seine River and includes two islands called the *Île de la Cité* and the *Île Saint-Louis*. The average temperature is 59 degrees Fahrenheit, and there are a lot of sudden rain showers."

My classmates are actually paying attention. Maybe it's because their mouths are so happy from the chocolate. Even Mr. Finncrisp is half-smiling at me as he chews.

"Paris has twenty neighborhoods called *arrondissements*, and all of them have a number assigned—one through twenty. The city has an awesome train network with 380 stations." I turn to Mr. Finncrisp's desk and pick up the train map I bought in Paris. I open it and walk up and down the aisles so that people can see it clearly. I smile as I watch the kids enjoying their croissants. "Education is a big part of Paris. There are 170,000 teachers or professors, and there are 2.9 million children and students in 9,000 grade schools, high schools, and colleges and universities."

I'm so glad I went to Paris to experience the culture even for a brief moment. I feel like I really know what I'm talking about because I was actually breathing real Parisian air, eating real French pastry, and sipping *café au lait*.

"Cafés have been a big part of the culture since Café Procope opened in 1689. I really enjoy the *café au lait*, which is coffee with milk. I wasn't allowed to serve you coffee, but I went ahead and made a recipe card for all of you with the chocolate croissant on one side and the *café au lait* on the other."

I can tell that the croissants are a huge hit because even X smiled at me. That's the first time he's ever smiled at me. It's amazing what chocolate can do!

"Thank you, Ms. Calderón. Time's up."

Mr. Finncrisp has his arms crossed and his half-smile is gone, probably because he knows I went way beyond book research. (He doesn't have any idea how far beyond I went!) I know he liked some parts of the report because I saw him stick the recipe card in his pocket before he called on the next kid. I'm also secretly giggling because he has chocolate smudged on the right side of his mouth.

"Guadey, I'm home!"

Guadey is sitting on the back porch writing at her special table. The sharp smells of spearmint and peppermint from her window garden hit me right inside my nose, so it tickles a little. I walk over to her and give her a kiss on the cheek.

"How did your report go today?" she asks.

"It was awesome! Hurley helped me pass out the croissants, Mr. Finncrisp took a recipe card and had chocolate on his face, and even X half-smiled at me! I think I'm getting an 'A'!"

"Wow! It sounds like a perfect day."

"It really was. How was your day? What are you working on?"

"I'm getting ready for a special seminar I'm teaching next week. I'm focusing on two poets: Ruth Stone and Lucille Clifton—these women have wisdom from another time, and I think my students really need to appreciate that. Do you understand what I mean?"

"I guess."

"You just guess?"

"Well, I don't really remember their poems."

"Selma, did you forget *all* the studying we did in Philadelphia?"

"Well, no ... maybe ... kind of. It's just that there's so much new fun stuff here in Chicago, plus when I went to Paris, I learned so much about—"

"You went to Paris?"

"Um, yeah ... in my mind."

"Selma Calderón. You know I know when you're not telling the truth. When did you go?"

I shift from foot to foot. "It was on Friday—I left during lunch and only missed one class. And I was doing the research for my city report for Mr. Finncrisp's class."

Guadey inhales and exhales, takes off her purple-framed glasses, and rests her fists on her tightly shut eyes. Then she drops her hands on the table and looks at me.

"Well, my dear, you know traveling isn't permitted during a school day and that you *have* to tell me where you go. You shouldn't be traveling by yourself."

My right shoulder blade tenses up. "I'm sorry, Guadey. Sometimes I just get so excited."

"I know, sweetie," she says. "But it's for your own safety. I don't want you getting stuck somewhere I can't find you."

"Okay, okay, I know. I really am sorry." My stomach sinks like it's filled with a pile of rocks.

"All right, now why don't you just sit by me while I prepare next week's lessons."

"But I just got home. Can't I watch some TV or go outside? I have to do my own homework soon. If I sit with you now, it'll be like doing double homework."

"Maybe you should have thought of that before you went abroad without telling me. You're lucky I'm not canceling Hurley's visit tomorrow."

Man, why didn't I just keep my mouth shut?

"Selma, this isn't homework, this is soul work. Poetry is meditation, and poets are the athletes of language. You need to exercise those soul muscles, and this is as good a day as any to do it. Let's start with Lucille Clifton. This one is called "atlas.""

I pull a stool next to Guadey so that I can read the poem.

i am used to the heft of it
sitting against my rib,
used to the ridges of forest,
used to the way my thumb
slips into the sea as i pull
it tight. something is sweet
in the thick odor of flesh
burning and sweating and bearing young.
i have learned to carry it
the way a poor man learns
to carry everything.

"It sounds like he's got the world on his shoulders, Guadey."

"I know, that's because Atlas was a god who rebelled against the Titans and was banished and punished by having to hold the heavens on his shoulders."

"Wow, that sounds heavy."

"Yes, and sometimes, regular people feel a heavy weight too." Guadey lifts up my chin, then takes both of my hands in hers. She looks straight into my eyes. "Your magic is a lot of responsibility. It's not just for eating *pain au chocolat* and changing water to iced tea."

My eyes widen because I realize Guadey knows about my little caffeinated spell at school last week.

"Yes, Selma," she says in a low voice. "I know things, even if I'm not with you. Too bad I didn't tune into you when you left for Paris."

I look down at the floor and pull my hands from Guadey's.

"Now," Guadey says, "I want you to write a poem. It can be about anything you want, and it'll be just for us. You don't need to show your friends at school. Got it?"

"Got it." I plop myself on Guadey's tiny red velvet love seat in her study.

Hmmm. What should I write about? I think I'll write about magic. I can write about how it's fun and also hard not to tell anyone about it. I pull my journal and my favorite black felt-tip pen from my backpack.

Spells make my fingers tingle!
Paris this week,
Bwindi next.
Guadey burns sage
smoking circles,
I feel cleaner now.
1441 West 18th,
our new home,
my trampoline

jumping up to heaven
heavy on
poor old Atlas.

This is a little bit harder than I thought, but still fun too.

I show my poem to Guadey, and she thinks it's a good start but that I need to work on it a little more. I know because I only spent a few minutes writing, and she wants me to be more thoughtful.

When I'm finished, she asks me about this trip to Bwindi I want to go on. I tell her it's sort of homework related because in science class we're learning about primates, so it would be a good idea to visit the mountain gorillas. Guadey actually agrees with my idea but tells me that next week isn't good for her, so I need to wait.

Waiting means patience. I don't have a lot of that. I wish I could conjure patience. Anyway, Hurley and I could just do a pre-trip planning visit because we need to check it out before we go on the real trip. I know I might get in trouble, but I think I can make it a really quick trip. I'm going to talk to Hurley about it and see what he thinks.

6

Bwindi Marbles

Selma

HOORAY! IT'S TUESDAY and I'm so excited the school day is finally over. Hurley and I pull our books from our lockers and walk home down 18th Street.

Halfway there, he turns to me and says, "I have some new marbles to show you. I won them in my last game in North Carolina."

"Cool! And I want to show you my notes and the Uganda guidebook I bought. I want to start planning a trip to Bwindi Impenetrable National Forest. Do you still want to go?"

Hurley stops walking and looks at me. "Selma, didn't you just get in trouble on Friday for going to Paris without permission?"

I turn around and face him. "Yes, but Guadey said I could go with her on this one. I was just thinking of an advance planning trip."

We continue walking in silence and cross Ashland Avenue, which is about three blocks from home. Hurley takes two marbles from his pocket and tosses them from one hand to the other. I know he plays with those marbles when he's nervous.

"I'll think about it, Selma."

"I'll tell you more when we get to my house, but it's like when the president visits a country abroad. There's an advance planning team to scope things out. That's all we'd be doing."

"And we would be going without permission too, Selma."

"I know, I know. Look, my apartment is right across the street, but first I want to introduce you to Mr. B. His real name is Mr. Beltrán. He owns this sewing machine shop. He's like the mayor of our block. He knows everyone."

I turn the small worn brass handle and we walk into his shop.

"Hi, Mr. B.!"

He comes out from behind the counter to greet us. Mr. B.'s gray and black curly hair matches his mustache.

"Hello, Selma. What are you up to today? And who's your new friend?"

Mr. B. pushes his silver wire-rim glasses up his

nose and extends his hand toward Hurley for a shake.

"This is my friend, Hurley. He moved here from Charlotte right when I moved here from Philly. He's a marble champ!"

Hurley shakes Mr. B.'s hand and his face lights up with a sunny smile full of straight teeth.

"Nice to meet you, Mr. B."

"The pleasure's all mine, Hurley. I played marbles as a boy in Mexico and I was pretty good. Maybe sometime you and Selma can stop by the store to show me some of your favorites."

I've never heard anyone show an interest in Hurley's marbles except me and, I suppose, Clare O'Connor. Hurley bounces up and down with excitement.

"Wow, Mr. B. I'll definitely bring some more marbles the next time. I only live a few blocks away, so I'm close by."

I don't want to ruin Hurley's moment, but I know Guadey has cooked us a special snack to be hot and ready now. "Excuse us, Mr. B., but we need to get home now."

"Sure, sure," he says. "Have fun!"

"Thanks!" we both say waving.

We walk across the street and I fish my keys out of my backpack, unlock the door, and walk in.

Guadey hears us and meets us at the front door.

"Hi, Guadey."

She bends down so that I can kiss her on the cheek. "Hi honey." Then she straightens as she greets Hurley. "Hello, Hurley. Welcome. It's so nice to officially meet you. Selma never stops talking about you." Guadey opens her arms to hug him.

He looks kind of surprised, but hugs her back. "Hi, Ms. Guadey. Thank you for letting me come over."

"It's our pleasure. Come back to the kitchen. The *chilaquiles* are nice and hot. They're Selma's favorite."

"Thanks!" Hurley says. "I'd love to try them."

We drop our backpacks just inside the front door and the three of us walk to the kitchen together as Hurley whispers, "They're not too spicy, are they, Selma? Do you think I'll like them?"

I scrunch up my face with a grin. "They might be a *little* spicy, but just try them. I want you to see why I love them so much."

Hurley nods. "Okay."

Hurley and I take our seats at the kitchen table, which is covered with a clear plastic tablecloth. I lean in and whisper. "I'm pretty sure Guadey got you a special treat for dessert—that is, if you like sweet potato pie."

Hurley beams with a big open-mouthed smile, "I

love sweet potato pie! That's my grandmother's specialty!"

Guadey smiles, winks at me, then serves the *chilaquiles* to us on bright orange plates. They look like scrambled eggs with tortilla chips mixed in. Two slices of avocado sit on the side of each plate, making it extra colorful.

Hurley says his grace quietly and I fold my hands, close my eyes, and wait for him to finish before I start eating. I want to watch him take his first bite. He puts a forkful in his mouth and smiles, then his eyes get big right before he swallows.

"The *chilaquiles* are good, Ms. Guadey, but I'm afraid they're a bit too spicy for me."

"Oh, no. I'm sorry, Hurley." She rushes to the counter and back. "Here, try this," she says, handing him half a long sandwich roll we call a *bolillo*. "Hold this in your mouth for a minute or two and drink some water. That should take the spice away. I'll get your *empanada de camote*."

Guadey pulls down a pretty blue dessert plate and hands it to Hurley. Meanwhile, I'm silent because I can't stop eating my *chilaquiles*, which in my opinion need a little *more* spice, but I'm glad Guadey made them mild for Hurley.

Hurley takes his first bite of the *empanada* right

in the middle where there's the most filling. "It's delicious, Ms. Guadey! Where do they sell these?"

"They make them every day right around the corner at El Nopal bakery."

"Really?" Hurley says, smiling with a big mouthful. He swallows, then says, "Cool! Sorry, my mom says not to talk with my mouth full, but it's *so* good."

Once Hurley and I finish, I take our plates to the sink. I'm excited to go outside and talk more about Uganda.

"Guadey, thanks for making my favorite and for buying Hurley's surprise. We're going to play marbles out back on the patio now."

"You're welcome, honey. Enjoy."

Hurley and I walk across the back porch where Uli is lounging on the trunk against the wall. "That's Uli, our cat. He's a cream point Siamese so he's super smart."

"Wow, I never saw one of those before. He looks like vanilla ice cream with a touch of caramel."

Uli flicks his tail like he knows we're talking about him. I lead Hurley down eight steps to our back patio. There's a wooden swing under our back porch that fits two people, and then most of our backyard is a big, smooth square block of cement.

"Wow, Selma! This is perfect for marbles! Do

you have some chalk so we can draw a circle?"

"Yep. It's right here under the swing."

"I'll draw it," Hurley says. "I know what size it needs to be."

"Okay." I look at Hurley and smile. Like I would ever try to draw a circle for marbles in his presence. He's always in charge of marbles and it's fine with me. I'm still learning to play and honestly, I'm not very good. But it makes Hurley really happy so I just follow his lead and do the best I can. Once Hurley draws the circle, kneels down, and sets up his shot, I decide it's time to talk about our plans.

"Hey, Hurley."

"Yeah, Selma?"

"So can we talk about our research for the trip to Uganda?"

Hurley is focusing on a shot and not really listening to me. I wait until he's done, get down on my knees the way he taught me, and take my shot. Then right before he aims again, I touch his hand. "Hurley, did you make up your mind about our advance planning trip?"

Hurley looks down at the marbles and then up at me. He kneels down, takes his shot, and misses. Then he scrunches up his face. "Actually ... I have a bad feeling about it."

I kneel down for my shot. I'm not focused on the game at all now. "We can keep it very short. I just want to see the mountain gorillas. I was reading on the African Wildlife Foundation website that there are less than nine hundred left in the whole world and that a lot of them live in Uganda." I let the marble fall from my hand.

"That's a slip, Selma. Next time, skip kneeling and try bombing." Hurley is constantly using "marbles lingo." I now know that bombing is when I just drop my marble rather than shoot it. I kind of like it that way; it's better than kneeling all the time.

Hurley's next shot is awesome and complicated. He makes it perfectly. He stands and thrusts both fists in the air. "Yes!"

"So, what do you think, Hurley?" I ask again.

"Well, it does sound cool to see the mountain gorillas. I was getting curious when we read about them in science class."

"And ...?"

"Okay, Selma, I'll go, but I'm telling you right now, if we get caught, I'm saying you made me go."

"Fair enough. We can go a week from this Friday after school. I want to go sooner, but I think I need to wait a little since I just took that unauthorized trip to Paris. Let's plan for you to tell your mom you're coming over again, and I'll tell Guadey I'm going over to your house to play marbles."

Hurley agrees and we keep playing marbles, but all I'm thinking is *Bwindi. Bwindi. Bwindi.*

I spend the rest of the week, most of the weekend, and the following week researching Bwindi Impenetrable National Forest. I find out that we can stay in *bandas*—which are small huts—in the park, kind of like camping. We can also stay several hours away in Kabale. I research local foods too and learn tons more about the mountain gorillas. Finally, Friday arrives.

We meet next door to my apartment at Café Jumping Bean after school to go over our plans. The café is on the corner of 18th and Bishop Street. It's pretty much just one small room with two walls of windows. I'm sitting at a table facing 18th Street so Hurley will see me right away. Once he spots me, he waves and comes in. I'm already writing in my journal and sipping my favorite mango *licuado* (that's a smoothie) with extra cinnamon sprinkled on top.

"Hi, Hurley."

He takes the seat across from me and pulls two marbles from his pocket. He's already rubbing them together in his hand.

"Hi, Selma," he says, then leans across the table and whispers, "I'm nervous about this whole thing. What's going to happen? What if we get separated?"

"We can't, Hurley. I haven't told Guadey, but I've been practicing short trips around the apartment with Uli." I try to distract him by talking about the marbles in his hand. "Are those new marbles?"

"Yeah, I stopped by Mr. B.'s on the way here to show him a few from my collection and he gave me two of his favorites. But wait, Selma, I'm still nervous. Uli is a cat. I'm a lot bigger. And traveling around your apartment is way different than going to Uganda."

"I know, but you're both beings, not objects, so we'll be okay." Hurley is making me nervous and my underarms are feeling sweaty even though I'm drinking something cold. "So, Hurley, what did you pack?"

"Pack?"

"Yeah, what are you bringing with you?"

"My marbles."

"Oh, of course. What was I thinking? Well, here's what I packed: a head lamp, my notebook, a thermos full of iced tea, three of my favorite felt-tip pens, my camera, two dark chocolate bars—one of them with almonds—and $32.37 from my saltwater taffy bank."

"Wow! You packed a lot more than I did. I thought you said this was going to be a really quick trip."

"It will be. I just like to have my favorite things with me. So here's the plan: We'll go to the back patio, and then I'll do the spell."

Hurley shrugs his shoulders. "Okay, let's just get it over with."

We walk out of the café and instead of going to my front door, we go around to the back alley. I use my key to open the padlock on our back gate. We tiptoe across the cement square where we play marbles and over to the wooden swing under the back porch. I'm wearing my backpack strapped on the front of me so that I can lean back in the swing. It's more comfortable to do the spell that way. Hurley has his leather marble bag hanging on his wrist. We sit next to each other on the swing with our arms interlocked at the elbows.

I look at Hurley. "It's going to be great and we'll make it quick! Ready?"

Hurley takes a deep breath and exhales. "Ready."

I start the spell.

Locking arms,
swinging slow,
take us where we want to go.

Mountain primates,
hills so green,
Uganda forest,
please be seen!
Cucalacas!

We land in the back of what looks like a Land Rover. It's dark because there aren't any lights on the road. There's only moonlight and I can see stars. What went wrong?

"Um, Selma. You didn't tell me it would be nighttime in Uganda."

"Oh, uh ... well, Hurley, I didn't know. I mean ... whoa."

We're bouncing along a road that winds up around a mountain. I am really sweating now. I grab Hurley's hand. I don't know if I'm trying to reassure him or myself. Either way, this is crazy. What on earth was I thinking? Who's driving us? I better find out.

"Hello sir. Are we almost there?"

The driver glances at me in the rearview mirror. "Hello, Miss Calderón. How are you holding up?" He answers me like I've been there the whole time and didn't just appear in the back of his vehicle.

"Oh, just fine. I'm sorry, though, will you please tell me your name again?"

"It's Patrick. Remember we talked about St. Patrick and how my mother liked his story?"

I look at Hurley. He has tears in his eyes and doesn't let go of my hand. I whisper to him, "I'm sorry. I'll figure a way out, I promise."

"Oh, yeah. Gee, Mr. Patrick, how much longer until we get to Bwindi?"

"Well, you're going to need to stay the night in Kabale, since the *bandas* are all occupied. And let's see, we've been on the road from Kampala for about four and a half hours, so we have another hour or two to go. All these trucks. Smugglers you know, from Zaire."

Zaire? That can't be right. When I researched the mountain gorillas' habitat, it said the gorillas ranged between Rwanda, Uganda, and the Democratic Republic of Congo ... wait, that used to be called Zaire.

"Zaire? You mean the Democratic Republic of Congo?"

Hurley's body shakes with fear and his hand is sweaty. Or it might be my hand. I'm trying not to cry because I don't want Hurley to start crying too. The Land Rover is hugging the side of the mountain. There are no streetlights like in Chicago. The only brightness comes from the headlights of our vehicle and the ones from oncoming eighteen-wheelers flying by at scary speeds. Hurley leans over and whispers to me, "Selma, do something."

Mr. Patrick looks in the rearview mirror and tilts his head in confusion. "No, I'm talking about Zaire. This has all happened since the war in Rwanda. The Hutus and Tutsis ... you know ... it was a massacre. They have no supplies left. Even the coffee crop was almost wiped out. Some say at least 500,000 people died, probably even more."

"But it's been more than twenty years since the war."

"What? Miss Calderón ..."

"Please call me Selma. I'm only ten."

"Okay, Selma ... it's 1996. Would you be confusing this war with another?"

Hurley and I look at each other in panic. I squeeze his hand. He's whimpering and tears are streaming down his cheeks.

I swallow and wipe a tear that's escaping from my eye. "Oh, right, I just got my dates confused."

Hurley grips his bag of marbles on his lap with his other hand. How did I mess up this spell so badly? We went to the right location but we didn't land in the right time. This is all my fault. If I messed up the spell to get here, I don't know if I can do it right to get us home. What if we can't get back to

Chicago? We've only been gone for an hour, but who knows if it's a real hour back home.

When will Guadey and Hurley's mom start to worry? My chest is tight. I'm having trouble breathing. I need to focus on something else. Hurley finally lets go of my hand and furiously rubs two marbles together, making a squeaky scraping sound. I take my chocolate bar out of my backpack and count how many almonds are in it by running my finger along the back of the bar. I don't know why this gives me comfort but it does.

We both watch out the window where we can barely see anything except dark green mountains and oncoming headlights from tractor-trailers. After almost two hours, I've counted twelve trucks that have passed us with barely an inch between vehicles. Patrick stops when we get to a small town. He pulls in front of a beige two-story building. The sign says "Hotel" in peeling red paint.

"Okay, we made it to Kabale. Here's your hotel. You two can grab dinner downstairs and then get some rest. I'll pick you up at 5:00 a.m. so we can drive to Bwindi, and then you can go with the first climbers at 7:00 a.m."

Hurley's face is stained with tears as he climbs out of the car. He speaks to Patrick for the first time. "Thank you, Mr. Patrick. Have a good night."

"You're welcome, Hurley. I'm glad to hear your voice. You didn't look too good back there. Lots of folks get carsick on that road, but you'll feel better after a nice meal. I know the owners here so don't worry. They'll take good care of you."

I swing my backpack onto my right shoulder and shake Mr. Patrick's hand. "Thank you for getting us here safely and for coming to get us tomorrow. We'll be ready!" I try to smile at him, but the smile doesn't reach my eyes. I'm so exhausted and hungry by this point, all I want to do is sit in the restaurant and apologize to Hurley over and over. *And* I have to figure out how to get us home.

"Take care you two," Patrick says. "I called ahead when the *bandas* were sold out and reserved a room for you with two double beds."

"Thank you," I call out as Mr. Patrick drives away.

We walk to the restaurant and find a table. "I'm so sorry, Hurley. I know I can get us home. I just know it." But I'm actually not so sure.

"How do you know, Selma? I thought you had the spell to get us to the mountain gorillas figured out. And what about my mom? She's going to be so worried."

"Gosh, Hurley. I don't know what went wrong.

I'm suspecting—or hoping anyway—that the time travel part means we're not missed for the same amount of time in Chicago."

He looks at me and rolls his eyes. "I don't know how that makes any sense, but I'm too tired to argue about it or try to understand it."

I don't know how *any* of this makes sense. How could Patrick remember a conversation we'd had earlier about his name? How could we just appear in the back of his truck? Why doesn't it seem odd that two kids are traveling alone at night to see the mountain gorillas?

My voice cracks as I say, "How about we eat first and discuss our next move?" I spot a menu painted on the wall across from us. "Oh look, Hurley, we can have roast chicken and *matoke*."

"What's *matoke*?"

"It's sort of smashed-up plantains, like bananas. I've always wanted to try it."

Hurley gives me his best "yuck" face. "Mashed bananas? Sounds like baby food."

"We might as well order something. We can plan things while we eat."

"Okay."

The waiter comes over to take our order.

"Good evening. What would you like tonight?"

"We'll each have the roasted chicken with *matoke* and two bottles of Krest."

"Okay, thank you," the waiter responds and heads toward the kitchen.

"What's Krest?" Hurley asks.

"It's a lemon-lime soda," I say.

"Oh, that sounds good."

We sit in silence as our stomachs growl. We're so happy when our plates arrive that I join in this time as Hurley says his grace, silently praying we'll find our way home soon.

Hurley takes a bite of the chicken and then the *matoke*. "Hey, this doesn't taste bad at all," he says with half a smile.

My shoulders relax a little. I can think a bit more clearly now that I'm eating and no longer on that dark bumpy road. "I told you, Hurley. So now we know what to order when we come with Guadey."

"Don't count on me coming for the real trip, Selma. Even if Guadey can do the spell correctly, I think I just want to stay in Chicago from now on."

I look down at my plate and move the chicken around with my fork. Normally, I'd list a bunch of reasons he should think about going on more adventures with me, but at this point, I have absolutely nothing to say. I'm just so upset I messed up.

While we eat, we decide on our plan—to try a spell in the morning once we arrive at the park, since that was supposed to be the destination for the original spell. After we're finished eating, I pay for everything, grateful that the restaurant happily accepts the dollars I brought from my saltwater taffy bank. When we leave the restaurant and walk to the front desk, I find out Patrick already paid for our rooms. Well, that makes two things that have gone right for us, which is better than the zero it was before.

We walk up to our room on the second floor. We decide to stay up all night playing marbles. Neither of us thinks we'll be able to sleep in a strange place. After only one game, though, Hurley is losing his balance on his knees and I can no longer keep my eyes open, so we each climb into our beds and fall asleep.

There's a knock at the door at 5:00 a.m. It's Patrick. "Selma, Hurley, are you awake? Let's hit the road."

I sit up as soon as I hear the knock and then lie. "Yes! We'll be down in five minutes!"

"Hurley, wake up! We have to go. Let's try to get home."

Hurley is groggy, but as soon as he hears

"home," he bolts upright and jumps out of bed. He even slept with his shoes on. "Let me use the bathroom and then I'll be ready."

I take my turn in the bathroom after Hurley. When I'm in there, I give myself a good look in the mirror. "You have to figure this out, Selma. You have to get home safely, or at least get a message to Guadey." When I leave the bathroom, backpack in hand, Hurley is waiting for me with his marble bag hanging from his wrist.

"Let's go, Selma. We're going to get home now."

I swallow, look Hurley in the eye, and try to act sure of myself. "We will, Hurley. We will."

When we climb into Mr. Patrick's car, the first thing he asks is, "So how was your sleep?"

I answer with a smile, a real one this time. "It was just fine, Mr. Patrick. Thanks for asking. And thank you for paying for our room. That was really nice of you."

"My pleasure. It was included in the package you purchased."

I nod and smile, again with no idea how any of this makes sense.

After some more bumpy roads in the early morning darkness, the light is coming just as we arrive at Bwindi Impenetrable National Forest. Patrick drops us off at the end of the road near the *bandas*. Lush, wet greenery is all around us. It almost feels like the rainforest from the morning dew (not that I've ever been to the rainforest). As I climb out of his dusty Land Rover, I say, "Thanks again for everything, Mr. Patrick. We'll see you soon."

"Good luck! I hope you don't have to hike far to see a family. Be sure to take lots of pictures. You'll need to follow this road until you see signs that say 'Wardens Gathering Point.' "

"Okay!" Hurley says, waving goodbye and sounding more excited than he's been for the whole trip. "We'll see you soon."

"Let's check in with the warden," I say, "to see if one of the gorilla families is nearby—if we don't have to do a long trek and can get a quick peek, I'll do the spell afterward."

"What? No, Selma. We're here. Let's just try to get home. Guadey and my mom are going to be worried."

"You're right, Hurley. But let's just start walking toward the forest so we're really in the park before we do the spell." I secretly hope we see a family because after all of this, I wish we could have one moment go as planned.

Hurley's steps are timed exactly with mine. Our shoes barely make any noise on the wet green leaves and grasses. The morning sunlight feels so gentle, I wish we could slow down for a moment and enjoy our surroundings. After all, we did make it to Bwindi. If there was ever a magical place in nature, this is it. As I keep pace with Hurley, I try to capture as much as I can with a few snaps of my camera.

"Selma, we don't have time for pictures now," Hurley says, tugging at my arm.

"I'm not slowing down, Hurley. Come on, just look around for a moment. It's so beautiful. The light is dancing on the leaves and vines. Look how you can see the dewdrops reflected by the sun."

Hurley keeps walking and so do I, but he does look up at the green canopy of trees. "Yeah, I guess you have a point. But I'm not interested in the dancing light. I just want to get home already." Hurley stops abruptly. "Wait. I hear something. Is that chewing? And it sounds like running water." He points, "Hey look, Selma, it's a buffalo, and there's a baby buffalo. Man, the mother's peeing an awfully long time."

This is our first sign of wildlife and it's not a good one. I quickly stick my camera into my backpack and put it on. I grab Hurley's arm and start pulling him up a hill in the opposite direction.

"Um, Hurley, let's go. Now."

"Why? She's not bothering us."

"Hurley, buffalos, they're not so friendly, especially when their babies ..."

Oh no. The buffalo's looking right at us. She's stopped chewing. She's beginning to walk toward us. Now she's running straight at us! She's getting faster!

Now I'm crying and suddenly feel paralyzed with fear. Everything I've done wrong with this trip is ending with this. We're going to die. Right now. Hurley yanks my arm and yells at me to run. I look at him wide-eyed and take off with him. I'm sobbing as I keep repeating, "I'm so sorry, Hurley. I'm so sorry!"

Hurley's pumping his arms so fast, he's getting way ahead of me up the hill. Suddenly I hear him say, "Dang it! I dropped my marbles." He turns around and yells, "Selma! Do the spell now!"

I have to stop crying and pull it together. I've never done a spell while running for my life. Here's goes:

Holding hands,
Wishing hard,
gray cement
my backyard.
Guadey's touch,
Take us quick
Feel our clutch,
Cuca ...

The mama buffalo is only five feet away. I can hear her snorting and feel her coming closer. I can even smell her wet fur. Oh gosh, why did I turn around? She's furious and there's snot flying out of her snout.

"Keep running, Hurley. The spell's not working!"

We both run through a freezing cold stream, and our clothes get soaked to our thighs. My boot gets stuck in the mud under a broken branch. There are a bunch of sticks and branches to jump around and over, and I'm struggling to keep up with Hurley. "I'm sorry! I'm sorry! I'm sorry!" I yell. I pull my foot loose just as I see Hurley's whole body lift off the ground, and then I realize I'm being lifted too.

I hear Guadey's voice.

Spirits round
and spirits flow,
forgive the children's
magic show.
Into the present
from this soil brown,
take us safely
to Chi-town!
Salamalanunca!

7

Making Up

Selma

I CAN'T GET OUT OF BED. I'm so exhausted. I'm almost more terrified of facing Guadey than I was of the mama buffalo. I'm in so much trouble. I didn't even get to say goodbye to Hurley because Guadey transported him home right from Bwindi. I bet he's so upset about losing his marbles and, of course, about when I ripped a hole in time and put our lives in danger. When we got home last night, Guadey told me she may freeze my powers and that I'm grounded for an indefinite period of time. I hope it's not for life.

The only comfort is that even though we were gone overnight by Uganda's time, something about the time travel meant that in Chicago, we were only gone a few hours. I don't know how that worked, but Guadey told me she started getting worried when she hadn't heard from me by dinner. Then she put out her magical feelers and "tuned into my channel."

What a great day it would have been, trekking to see a whole family of mountain gorillas. I want to write a poem to Guadey to tell her I'm sorry and see if she'll forgive me. I hope she won't freeze or take away my magic powers like she says she might. And poor Hurley. What can I do to get his marbles back?

I hop out of bed and dump all my savings from my saltwater taffy bank onto my bedspread. I used most of my money to pay for dinner on our trip, but I count the remaining dollars and all the change. I have $7.36 left, plus my lucky two-dollar bill framed on my wall. I better give that to Hurley. That will make $9.36 to pay for new marbles. Only I'm not sure buying him new ones will help or change anything because he won those back in North Carolina. They're irreplaceable. And I can't believe he also lost the ones Mr. B. just gave him. I feel awful.

I wish Guadey could use her magic to get them back, but she already told me last night that I did something dangerous when I went back in time, and for her to go back and get the marbles could make it worse.

All I can do now is try to make it up to Hurley and Guadey. I'm going to call Hurley right now. I'm lucky I have my emergency cell phone in my room. Too bad I didn't have a magical version of this in Uganda.

I dial his number, but my stomach is all fluttery and my eyes are filling up with tears. I hope he doesn't hang up on me. I need to at least face him over the phone. It's ringing. He's answering.

"Hello?"

"Hi, Hurley. It's me."

"Oh, hi. Sorry, but I don't think I want to talk."

Now tears are actually coming out of my eyes. "But ... okay. I understand. I just want to say I'm sorry again. Sorry for almost getting us killed and lost in time. And sorry for making you lose your marbles. Can you ever forgive me?"

Hurley lets out a big sigh. "I thought you said you understood when I said I didn't want to talk."

"I do." I pace the perimeter of my tiny room.

"Then I'm going to hang up now. Bye."

"Bye."

I leave the phone on my desk, crawl back under the covers, and curl into a ball against the wall at the top corner of my bed. I cover my head with my pillow and sob—big snot-filled, hole-in-my-heart sobs. Did I just lose my best friend? After a while, I start taking deep belly breaths until I can do three in a row without any hiccupy sobs.

If he won't talk to me, I have to do something. I can't give up on us. We're a team. I kick off the covers and stare at the painting on my ceiling. Everything is bright and happy up there. I have to use my brain. I'm going to write him a letter. That way he can read it when he's calmed down a little. I get out of bed and pull out my craft supplies. On green construction paper, I draw a frequent marble game card. It's a rectangle with a bunch of squares in it. Each square is worth one game. The letter I write to go with it says:

Dear Hurley,

I'm so sorry I put your life in danger. And I'm so sorry I made you lose your marbles in Uganda. I know they were very special to you because you won them in North Carolina. And if Mr. B. asks, you can tell him it's my fault his favorite marbles are missing. Maybe leave out the part about the magic if that's ok.

I wish I could go back and get them for you, but for now I'm grounded. So the best I can do is give

*you my savings—$9.36 including my lucky $2
bill so you can buy new marbles. Also, I made
you a frequent marble champ card. You can ask
me to play marbles anytime and I always have to
say yes. There's even a bonus square with a triple
game in the middle. I hope you will still be my
friend.*

YFF,
Selma

Today is Saturday and Monday morning can't come
fast enough. Even if Hurley won't talk to me, I'm
going to give him the money, the letter, and the
marble champ card when I see him first thing in
homeroom. I'm not ready to face Guadey, but I have
to eat some breakfast sooner or later. The last thing I
ate was chicken and *matoke* in Kabale hours ago.

I shuffle to the kitchen in my pj's and socks.
Guadey is sitting at the kitchen table with a big
paper that measures the width of the table. She has
handwritten a numbered list of chores. There are
108 in total. Her hair is a mess. She has black circles
under her eyes and she's holding a cup of tea
between both hands.

"Good morning, Selma," she says coldly. "What
do you want to eat?"

"Anything, Guadey." I sit and fold my hands in my lap.

"Then how about pouring a bowl of cereal. I'm too tired to cook."

"Okay," I say.

She shakes her head at me. "Honestly, Selma, what part of my instructions about waiting to go to Uganda didn't you understand?"

I look at my hands, then at her. "I'm sorry, Guadey. I was just so curious. I was going to scope things out before our family trip."

Guadey crosses her arms and leans forward on the table. "Scoping things out is the same as taking a trip without permission, Selma. *And*, you endangered your best friend."

I put my head down. "I know." I scoot back my chair and walk to the cabinet to get cereal and a bowl. I grab a spoon from the drawer and set all three down on my side of the table. I start toward the fridge to get the milk but stop next to Guadey's chair. I begin to cry. Guadey pulls me into her arms and starts crying too.

"I can't lose you, Selma. I almost lost you. First your mom, then you."

Wow, Guadey never talks about my mom. She must miss her as much as I do. She hugs me and I imagine a warm furry bear protecting me as her long hair tickles me.

"I know, Guadey. I'm sorry. I'm really, really sorry. I'll never do it again. But my mom was different. It was an accident. It wasn't her fault. This *was* my fault."

Guadey pulls me out of the hug, holds my shoulders, and looks at me. Her face is twisted up like her stomach hurts. "Your mom ... she ..."

"I know. It was the boating accident."

"No, she ... went missing."

She always says it that way, *went missing*. I wonder why.

"What about dad? You lost him too."

Guadey lets go of me and pulls a napkin from the stack on the kitchen table. She wipes her eyes and blows her nose. "Yes, I lost your dad too, at the same time. It's just that your mom and I are like sisters."

I nod.

"But we're talking about you right now. You could have been lost in time—or worse, killed by a buffalo. Both you *and* Hurley could have died."

"I know." I go get the milk from the fridge and walk back to my seat looking at the tile floor, wondering why she said *are* like sisters in the present tense, like my mom is still alive. But I don't mention it. Instead I say, "I can't believe I risked my life ... and Hurley's too."

"Well," Guadey says, "you know there are consequences." She points down at the list of chores on the table. "I also want you to write a poem so you can reflect on your actions."

I nod and pour the cereal and milk into my bowl, knowing there's no getting out of it.

Guadey pushes her chair from the table. "I'm going to take a nap since I didn't sleep too well last night. When I wake up, I want to see a draft of your first poem." She slides a pile of blank paper across the table. "Okay?"

"Okay."

I inhale my cereal. I'm still hungry, so I pour myself another bowl. Uli jumps up on Guadey's chair and watches me eat.

"Uli, I wish you could help me with my chores."

He flicks his tail at me.

Once I'm finished with my second bowl, I push it toward Uli so that he can have the leftover milk. I might as well start writing. I can't bear to think about the details of the last day, so I'm going to look at my list of chores for inspiration. I know Guadey wants me to write about Uganda, but right now all I

can think about is this list I have to get done. So I try
a poem about chores.

> soap bubbles swirl a fortune
> tell me what to do
> wash the plates
> sweep the floor
> spin a spell
> what's true?
> unload groceries
> plan a meal
> my restaurant's far away
> right now
> I wish for chore angels
> please bring your brooms and stay

When I walk into homeroom on Monday morning,
Clare O'Connor is setting up her chair alongside
Hurley's desk. She shows him a ring on her finger.
Hurley cups his chin in his hands with his elbows on
his desk, looking uninterested, but when he sees me
approaching, he leans in, nods, and looks more
closely. He even shifts his shoulder toward her so
that his back is to me. That makes me walk faster
toward both of them.

I set my backpack next to Hurley's desk. "Hi, Clare. Hi, Hurley."

Clare smiles at me. "Hi, Selma. Do you want to see my Celtic knot ring? It's very special. It came from my grandmother in Ireland."

I look at the ring on her hand. The knot looks like it's made of gold snakes.

"It's nice, Clare. But, um ... do you think I can talk to Hurley for a few minutes?"

"Sure." She shrugs and carries her chair three rows up to her desk.

After a moment, Hurley turns around to face me. He still hasn't said hello. My legs feel kind of wobbly. This is crazy. How can I be this nervous talking to Hurley?

I reach down into the front pocket of my backpack and pull out the envelope filled with the money, letter, and frequent marble champ card. I speak quickly in a whisper. "Here, Hurley. This is for you. I know you may not want to talk to me ever again. But please open this envelope and think about being my friend again." My voice cracks when I say "friend."

"Thanks." Hurley takes the envelope, unzips his backpack, and drops it in—all without looking me in the eye.

Then he opens his math workbook and starts tackling a word problem. Hurley doesn't even like math. I stand there for another minute and watch him figure out the problem, scribbling numbers on the page. He still doesn't look up. I reach out to pat him on the shoulder, then change my mind and pull my hand back. "Okay," I say, "I'll see you later."

He erases a number in his book, keeps his head down, and murmurs, "See you."

I walk back to my desk and sit down. The minute I'm gone, Clare dashes back and starts talking to Hurley again. What's up with that? I feel so alone without Hurley, and there's this knot bunching up in my shoulder blade. I wish Clare would find somebody else to be her new friend.

Two school weeks have gone by since Uganda. It's Monday morning and I'm up to 39 chores completed. Since I've been great at crossing things off my list, Guadey is giving me a chore-free day today. Last week, Hurley started saying "hi" to me in the morning in homeroom, and we had a few conversations in the hallway. Today I'm going to take a risk and invite Hurley over after school. Guadey thought it was a good idea.

I get to homeroom early so I can start talking to Hurley before Clare comes into the picture. I want to dislike her, but she's so nice all the time. And I can't exactly blame her for wanting to be friends with Hurley. As soon as I see Hurley walk into the classroom, I jump up and follow him to his desk.

"Hi, Hurley."

"Hi, Selma."

"How've you been?"

"Okay. My mom never found out about Uganda. I'm guessing Guadey did something to make that happen." He takes his backpack off, hangs it on the back of his chair, and sits down.

"Oh, yeah, I think she told your mom we had dinner and were working on a school project, and that you forgot to call."

"Oh." Hurley pulls out his math book but doesn't open it.

I'm so anxious I'm shifting from foot to foot. Hurley tilts his head at me. I've never been so nervous to talk to my best friend. At least I hope he's still my best friend.

"Guadey said I can invite you over after school. Do you want to come over? We can start punching holes in your frequent marble champ card."

"Just marbles, right? No trips?"

"No trips. Just marbles, iced tea, and dark chocolate bars. And we can even get you an *empanada de camote*." I smile. I feel less nervous now that I said that.

Hurley gives me a double thumbs up. "Great! I'll send my mom a text and see if it's okay. If she says yes, I'll meet you at the Blue Kangaroo Laundromat parking lot after school."

Yippee! He said yes. It looks like we're still friends after all. I'm so relieved, I could cry.

Hurley and I had a great time yesterday. Now that it's been a little over two weeks since that crazy Friday in Uganda, things are finally back to normal. We sit together at lunch every day, and we still have B-O-R-I-N-G Mr. Finncrisp's social studies class, but now the whole school is getting ready for the Chicago Marathon. Every year it takes place on the second Sunday in October, which is coming up this weekend. The marathoners will run right in front of my apartment. We plan on making signs to support the runners that say, "You got this!" and "There's no place like the finish line!" and "Run like a Kenyan!"

I looked up the winners from the last three years and they've been from Kenya every time. I found an article with a scientific theory about why Kenyans from the Rift Valley win. It said that it's not just the training; scientists have found that living at a high altitude and walking and running a lot as part of their daily life, like to and from school, helps them grow into winners. That's got to be farther than I walk! And they don't eat any junk food. This makes me curious. If Guadey ever does take me to Uganda to see the mountain gorillas, maybe we can also visit Kenya and go running with marathoners! Or at least maybe I can visit the Rift Valley, even if I can't keep up with the runners.

Today is Thursday and Hurley and I are meeting after school across the street at Harrison Park to pretend we're training for the marathon. As I cross the street to meet him in the middle of the soccer field, I see him munching on the other half of his peanut butter and strawberry sandwich from lunchtime. He's probably trying to get extra energy to win. He finishes eating, stands up, and then stretches his arms above his head, smiling at me. We're both wearing hats and gloves in addition to our jackets. We're the only kids in school using winter stuff already because it's not cold for kids who already lived here before.

"Hi, Hurley."

"Hi, Selma. How many miles are you doing today?"

"Oh, I'm up to eighteen miles. How about you?"

"I'm going to do twenty today." He hops up and down on his toes, warming up.

We don't actually run anywhere close to that, but it's always fun to pretend that we train like real athletes.

"Cool! Want me to time you?" I ask.

"Yeah, sure. You can conjure up a bike and ride alongside me."

"How about if I ride a giant sea turtle next to you?" I grin picturing the amazing sea turtles I read about in science class.

"A sea turtle? Aren't they kind of slow?"

"Mine have special powers ... floating powers ... flying powers!"

Hurley's face freezes. "Selma, don't go making any magic sea turtles appear."

"I know, Hurley. I'm just pretending."

"Good. Let's run the perimeter of the soccer field, and then we'll count that as our training." He pulls his hat lower over his ears. "I'll start us off. Runners take your mark. Ready, set, go!"

We're fast at the beginning, our backpacks bouncing on our backs. Hurley is breathing hard by the time we reach the other soccer goal. We still have to run to the other sideline and back to where we started.

"Come on, Hurley. We can do this. Let's sing to keep our breathing regular."

"Okay, let me start. You just follow my lead and repeat whatever I say."

I wonder how Hurley's going to lead the song when he's breathing so hard, but he starts singing one of those military songs I've heard in movies.

"I don't know but I've been told."

"I don't know but I've been told." I'm starting to breathe heavy now too.

"Selma girl is really bold."

I giggle. "Selma girl is really bold."

"When she says a spell just right."

Now I'm laughing, running, panting, and trying to repeat every line—all at the same time.

"When she says a spell just right."

"A boy named X might scream in fright."

"A boy named X might scream in fright."

I pump my arms up and down with a big smile.

Hurley keeps going. "Count on this today my friend."

"Count on this today my friend."

"We'll fight him to the bitter end."

"We'll fight him to the bitter end."

We're almost to the other soccer goal and Hurley is speeding up.

"Sound off! Now you say, 'One! Two!'" Hurley huffs.

"One! Two!"

"Three! Four! Bring it on down."

I repeat, "Three! Four!"

We've made it to the goal and Hurley points at me. "You say 'One! Two!'"

"One! Two!"

"Three! Four!"

Now we both stand in front of the goal panting while Hurley puts up his fingers one by one to cue me with the numbers. We sing as loudly as we can, "One, two, three, four!"

Hurley fist pumps the air and shouts, "Three, four!"

It was so much fun, I want to do another round ... just not the running part. "That was awesome, Hurley! You could be a poet!"

"Thanks! Let's go play marbles in front of the park district center before you have to head home. I still have seven games left on my marble champ card."

"You got it."

8

X Marks the Moo

Selma

IT'S SATURDAY MORNING, the day before the marathon. I'm standing on the 18th Street stop platform. Guadey has an all-day workshop at the university, so she's already left for the day. I'm taking the "L" to Harold Washington Library downtown so I have to take the train to the loop. That's where five different train lines all come together and go around in a circle toward a bunch of close-together stops in the middle of the city. It's cool that my stop is on 18th Street because my birthday's also on the 18th—of April, that is. This makes me think it's a good sign we chose to move here.

There are millions of pigeons. Okay, not millions, but *a lot* of pigeons hanging out on the platform where commuters have to stand. They're looking for doughnut scraps or any other food they can find. And they're not afraid of humans. I remember the first time taking the train by myself. I was distracted by a mural of a skeleton wearing a big straw hat with cherries and bananas hanging off the rim when my foot bumped into something soft and hard at the same time. It was a pigeon. I made the loudest "Aaaack!" sound ever and stood there shaking my arms and body, basically freaking out. He didn't even fly away. And no one who was waiting for the train reacted to the pigeons or to my yelling.

It seems like the people who wait for the train see so much of the same thing that they don't even see what's around them. A lot of people just keep their heads down looking at their phones. But I'm still in information-collecting mode and pay atten-tion to the sights, smells, and people around me. I carry an emergency cell phone, but I don't use it much. I'd rather take in the interesting things going on in the world. I guess I'm always going to be that way. And I like that about myself.

I'm on my way to the library because Guadey suggested I research poets like Maya Angelou and Virginia Hamilton Adair. But I'm not focusing on poets today. What I really plan to do is learn more about magic.

I know I've made some big mistakes, especially with Uganda, but I think it's because I don't know enough about magic and need to do my own studying on top of what Guadey taught me over the summer. She still hasn't taught me anything new since school started and it's already October. Ever since she found out about the iced tea trick at school and my trips to Paris and Uganda, it feels like she's afraid of what I might do if I know more. I guess I don't blame her. But I think if I learn more and practice, I'll be able to create spells for any situation and then never mess up again like I did with Uganda.

The sun is shining brightly today, but my earlobes are damp and cold—I thought it was going to be warmer so I didn't wear a hat. I feel a tickle on the back of my neck from the wind, and I hop up and down to stay warm. The train rail has started humming, which means it's coming. Yup, I was right! The automated voice says, "An inbound train from the Loop is arriving shortly."

Once the train arrives, I jump on and hear "doors are closing." The speakers always blast that message the minute the doors open, making it feel like there's no time to get on. There aren't many people in the train car since it's a Saturday. It's not like the early morning during the weekdays. That's when everyone is rushing to work and school, and they're all sleepy-eyed with their heads down looking at the *Chicago Tribune* or the *Sun-Times*, scanning their phones, or zoning out with earbuds stuck in their ears.

The train is quiet today partly because they're not announcing the stops. The speakers must not be working. But even when they are, the train is like a land where people have lost their voices. Nobody seems to like to talk, so they communicate through a nod to say, "Excuse me, this is my stop," or a tip of the head with the chin pointed forward to say, "How you doin'?" It's a commuters' zombie land, and I kind of like it.

I got the seat closest to the conductor in the front car, and as the train rattles on, I get a first view of the skyline with the Willis Tower, a dark shining monument in the middle of my new home. I like it here, but sometimes I miss Philly. It was easy to get a cheesesteak or a regular slice of pizza there. That's not the case in Chicago. Don't get me started about deep-dish pizza. It's a casserole, not a pizza. That's the only thing I don't like here. Well, that and the cold. And X. I wish he didn't go to my school.

Home makes me think about my parents. I can't really remember them. But I've always wondered about how they died, and why their boat had an accident. When Guadey and I were in the kitchen right after Uganda, Guadey acted weird when we talked about them. I feel like Guadey wanted to tell me something, then decided not to. I'm hoping as I learn more about magic, I can dig around and find out exactly what happened. I'm sure Guadey is hiding some part of the story. I feel it in my chest. Something about it is mysterious and I'm going to find out what it is.

We arrive at the library stop and I hop off the train. I'm so excited to be here that I run down the stairs of the train station. The library is practically connected to the station and it takes up a whole block. Just a few feet from the bottom of the stairs, I grip the long brass handle on the entrance door of the gigantic building. Before I left, I used Guadey's laptop to find the locations of the two books I want to check out, so I immediately go to the fifth floor. I walk down three aisles until I find two books by Valerie Worth: *The Crone's Book of Magical Words* and *The Crone's Book of Charms and Spells*. Now that I found those, I'm just going to wander a bit. I run my forefinger along the spines of the books—it's one of my favorite ways to discover new ones on the way to what I'm looking for. Wait, this one is interesting: *Reinventing My Magic* by Ulises S.

Caramelo. I take that one down from the shelf just for fun because the author spells his name exactly the way we spell Uli's name. I think three books should do it for now, so I head down to the third floor to check them out.

When I get home, Guadey asks to see the books I chose.

"What are these?" she asks. "Where are the ones by Maya Angelou? And what about *Ants on the Melon* by Virginia Hamilton Adair?" I stay quiet as she places the books next to her on the couch and props her feet up on the coffee table. Then she flips through each one as I sit on the carpet across from her petting Uli. Guadey chuckles when she sees the last book, *Reinventing My Magic.*

"What's so funny about that one?" I ask.

She closes it on her lap, leans forward, and says, "I know the author." Then she winks at Uli.

I look at Uli then back at Guadey. "How could you know the author? The book is really old. That doesn't make any sense."

Guadey piles all three books on the table between us and pushes them toward me. "I meant to say *I know of the author.* That was a lifetime ago."

I shrug my shoulders and pick up the books as Guadey shakes her head at me. "That wasn't quite the assignment I gave you, you know," she says as I dash off to my room with Uli trailing behind.

I'm surprised and happy that Guadey's not making me return the books right away. I was worried she might not let me study them, but I guess she didn't find anything to worry her, even though I didn't check out the books she asked me to get.

In my room I grab my journal and a pen from my desk, and then sit at the head of my bed against propped-up pillows. Uli stretches at the end of my bed, then lies down and watches me read. I sit cross-legged with *The Crone's Book of Magical Words* on my lap. The other two books are on my left side, and my journal and pen are on my right side so that I can make notes on the spells I want to learn.

Guadey hasn't pulled her wooden recipe box down from the top of the fridge for me since August. She said she would teach me more spells after I practice what I've already learned. I've thought about standing on a chair and sneaking a peek, but I know I won't be able to open the magical lock. I kind of don't blame her since I took two trips without permission.

I'm still not done with my chores either; I'm up

to 47 on the list of 108. But I really want to spend my time learning more spells and getting better at creating my own. Like now I'm wondering if I could change Uli into a magic sea turtle, just for maybe an hour, and then turn him back. That idea gets me a little nervous because something could go wrong, and I love Uli too much to let anything happen to him. Still, I'm more curious than nervous, so I'm going to add "shape shifting" to the list of areas I need to research in the future.

My top priority is to find ways to uncover the truth about my parents. I found one spell called "To Enlist the Elements' Aid for High Cause." After flipping through a few more pages, I switch to *The Crone's Book of Spells and Charms*. I find a spell named "Against Falsehood and Deception." There are some symbols that go with the spell—an eye, a snake, and flames. I could draw them on paper, but it would be cool to put them on something I could hold like a good luck charm. That spell could be a great way to find out the truth. I'm definitely coming back to this page.

I'm a little anxious about experimenting—and I definitely won't travel without permission ever again—but I keep reading and find another interesting spell. "Hey, Uli. Check this out: a spell to speed the hours. I wonder if that would help me to do my homework faster. Then I could have more time to create my own spells, investigate my parents' disappearance, and hang out more with Hurley— and I'd still technically be doing my homework without help! Wouldn't that be great?"

Uli flicked his tail at me. "No."

I drop the book on the bed.

"Uli, did you just answer me?"

Uli licks his paw and cleans his face. Then I hear him again.

"Perhaps."

"How cool! But ... your mouth isn't moving and I only hear you in my head, and you're a cat. Does Guadey know?"

"Of course she knows." He stands up now and walks toward the head of the bed. He sits right in front of me. "Humans!"

"What did you say?"

"Humans! You think you know everything. You rush through decisions and then wonder why things don't turn out as you planned. Cats have survived lots and lots of human mishaps."

I cross my arms on my chest. "I can't believe you're actually talking to me, but I get your point. You don't think this spell is a good idea."

Uli climbs onto me so that his front paws are balanced on my crisscrossed legs and his nose is level with mine. "Let's see. You got caught after your trip to Paris. Guadey had to save you and Hurley in Uganda. You made him lose his marbles and almost lost your friendship with him. Your track record is not good." Uli steps down from my legs, flicks his tail at me, and walks to the end of the bed.

I uncross my arms and flop my hands palms up on my knees. "Well, Uli, this doesn't involve any traveling, so I thought I'd just try it for a week."

"No."

My mouth is hanging open. "No?"

"That's right. No. You still haven't finished your chores list. Even if you don't have to do them every day now, you still have laundry, sweeping the cement out back, and planning the remaining dinners you're responsible for. Not to mention cooking them and doing the dishes. Do you really want more chores?"

"No."

I jump up and start pacing around my room. "Okay, fine, but if I could at least speed up homework or even my chores just for one week, then we might have more time to focus on dealing with X. I can't stand him." I stomp my foot twice with my fists balled at my sides and Uli barely moves. "He decided to pick on Hurley from his very first day of school when he started calling him 'Hail Baby,' one of the silliest names I've ever heard. I know Guadey doesn't want me doing magic in school, but ugh, he gets me so mad!" I clench my fists so hard my knuckles are white.

Uli's tail flicks faster back and forth. "The point of your magic is to hone your skills by sharpening your brain. But first you need to do the brain work. Use it—your brain—my dear. You and Hurley can come up with something together."

I take a deep breath and exhale loudly with a pout, making my lips vibrate. "Fine. I don't like it, but I guess I'll wait to spend more time with these spells. I better go do my homework since it's going to take longer now that I can't use magic."

Uli lies back down at the foot of my bed and turns his head toward me. "Actually, you are merely living with the consequences of not telling the truth, Selma. Take responsibility for your actions. You need to learn that lesson before you try one more spell."

My shoulders sink with the knowledge that he's right. "I get it, Uli. I'm telling the truth and only the truth from now on."

Uli curls his body into an oval, exhales through

his nose, tucks his head into his tummy, and closes his eyes.

Hurley and I decide to spend all of Sunday cheering on the marathoners. We get up extra early and walk a block from my apartment to a row of rectangular tables lined up along the curb. The tables are covered with bananas and blue paper cups filled with water. We get there just in time to see all the professional runners, and most of them are from Kenya! The race volunteers even give us free cowbells we can ring to help cheer them on. It's so fun! I take pictures of the Kenyan runners at the beginning and the stragglers at the end of the race. Lots of them jog or walk because our neighborhood marks mile 18 of 26.2 and they are *tired* by the time they get here. I also take photos of the sea of crushed blue water cups and banana peels on the ground.

Being a spectator makes me feel a little more like I belong in Chicago. I miss Philly sometimes, but with Hurley and Guadey, it's starting to feel like home.

The next day when I arrive at school, I see Hurley walking toward homeroom from the opposite end of the hallway. He stops at our lockers first. Ugh, X is behind him. What a way to start my morning. Oh man, he's going right for Hurley. Hurley pushes his head farther into his locker, then X takes his giant hand and slams Hurley's locker door so that it smashes into his head.

"Where's your marbles, Hurley? Where's your little girlfriend, Slimy Selma?"

"She's my friend, and she's not slimy," Hurley answers, glaring at X while rubbing the side of his head. I rush to Hurley's side. "I'm right here. Moooooo," I say.

X lowers his brow and sneers at us.

"Mooooooo." I poke Hurley, so he'll do the same thing. Then we both start saying, "Mooooooo."

By now there's a small crowd gathering around Hurley's locker. A few others start mooing at X too. Clare O'Conner is mooing the loudest.

"Okay, Calderón, what's up with the mooing?" X asks. "You been eatin' the grass over at Harrison Park?"

Some of the kids laugh nervously.

"Well, you know, from all those hamburgers you eat and all that time you spend around dead cows, I figured you'd be more comfortable hearing their language," I say.

The crowd laughs hard this time. I start mooing again. Then Hurley steps between me and X and starts with a real strong "Mmmmmmm" and winds up with a deep "oooooo." The crowd starts mooing again.

X clenches his fist. I've seen him pull a girl's hair before, but I've never seen him punch one, and I don't want to be the first. I haven't completely thought through this whole standing-up-to-the-bully thing. X's face is turning red. He pushes past Hurley and me and disappears down the hall. Everyone just keeps on mooing. Boy, are we lucky that his usual friends aren't around because they've been suspended for vandalizing Mr. Finncrisp's class-room. If they had been here, he might have started a real fight with me, Hurley, and everyone else mooing.

"Moo? Where'd you come up with that?" Hurley asks.

I shrug and smile. "Let's just say a furry friend made me prepare and think a little harder for our next encounter with X."

Hurley tilts his head at me and crosses his arms. "Well, it seemed to work this time, but when his friends get back from suspension, we're going to have to figure something else out. Maybe a spell?"

I stand with my mouth open, then push Hurley's

shoulder. "Why, Hurley Nathaniel Bartholomew Bingenworth, did I just hear you correctly?"

"No. Um, yes. Maybe." He smirks.

We walk back down the hallway to homeroom together now that the crowd has thinned out. I turn to Hurley. "Well, we've got to come up with something else because Guadey's got her eye on me. And I still have two weeks of chores, and she wants me to write more poems. Hey, maybe I'll write one about X. Then *much* later we can turn it into a spell." Hurley grabs my elbow and hurries me forward. "We'll see, Selma. I was just kidding about the spell, sort of. We better get to homeroom on time."

9

Water

Guadey

IT'S SATURDAY AND I wake up at 5 a.m.—that's an hour earlier than normal. The spirits tell me it's time to pull down the recipe box full of spells from the top of the fridge. I climb out of bed and head to the bathroom to wash my face and brush my teeth. I step into the kitchen, grab a glass, and pour fresh water from our pitcher. I slice a lemon and squeeze half of it into the glass. Then I add a pinch of cayenne pepper. I sit down at the kitchen table and slowly drink my morning tonic. It wakes up every part of me. Only then do I reach for the wooden recipe box.

The locking spell works on everyone but me, so opening it is as simple as opening any box without a latch. I flip through the spells until I find one to bind Selma's powers. I've been thinking about doing this since Uganda. Even if she means well, I think her curiosity is too strong to prevent her from practicing new spells at school. I'm okay with a little experimentation at home; after her trip to the library, she's bound to try a new spell or two. For now, though, my biggest concern is for her magic at school. I set the spell card down in front of me on the kitchen table, close my eyes for a moment, and visualize Selma happily walking down the hallway at school. Then I open my eyes and recite:

> *Spirits round*
> *sing Yemaya,*
> *the sea protects*
> *this child.*
> *Her learning halls*
> *are fortress bound,*
> *no girlhood magic*
> *to be found.*
> *Salamalanunca!*

Good. Now her powers won't work in school. I'm not going to tell her just yet, though. If she tries anything at school and finds her powers are frozen, I want to see if she comes to talk to me about it. The iced tea tricks are harmless, but I can see her temper rising around this X and her itchiness to try another trip.

In a way, I can't blame Selma for her natural curiosity. Her mother, Amelia, liked to do magic in school too. Back in Philly, we were classmates since in grade school. By high school, once the weather turned warm, we used magic once a week to transport ourselves to the beach in Ocean City, New Jersey. Since it wasn't very far away, we convinced ourselves we weren't breaking any big rules. Now that I'm taking care of Selma, I admit I can't believe I thought there were big rules or small rules.

At the beach, we'd have body surfing races to see who could ride the waves for the longest. Then we'd drink iced tea and eat Taylor pork roll with melted American cheese on soft rolls. After that, it was always a toss-up between boardwalk fries—if we could stuff them in—or Johnson's caramel popcorn. I always wanted to follow the salty with the taste of sweet caramel. We went all the way through high school without ever getting caught by our teachers.

The last time we went body surfing, Amelia clearly let me win—something she never did. I stood up in triumph at the shore, flipping my hair off my face. As I looked back at the ocean, at first all I saw was Amelia's black hair splayed out behind her. Then I realized she was facing someone. I could see her shoulders doing that cartoon-girl giggle. I stood there and watched her fall in love in the Atlantic Ocean—with a merman.

His name was Isaac. His brown eyes had a kind of golden glow. I could see that much from the shoreline. I walked back into the water toward them but didn't get close enough to hear them talking. When Isaac saw me approaching, he looked past Amelia at me, then shrugged his shoulders and tilted his head with his palms up as if to say, "I couldn't help it."

The following week, we took one more trip to the ocean together. On that trip, Isaac—with the love of Amelia—walked on human legs out of the water. This was the first time I officially met him. When I shook his hand, instead of saying "nice to meet you," he simply said, "thank you." I squinted my eyes and gave him a half smile. "You're welcome." I was confused and didn't know then what he must have known—that his love for Amelia would separate my best friend and me.

His dirty-blond hair still had some bright green seaweed matted in the back, the kind with the tiny bubbles you can pop like plastic packing material.

So the three of us went under the boardwalk to clean him up a little for outside-of-ocean life. We even conjured some clothes and sneakers. That next week, Isaac came back to high school with us as a senior-year transfer student and rented a room from an older woman in the neighborhood named Mrs. Pulaski. He worked early in the morning and after school in her Polish bakery for the cost of his room. He used to bring us *krusciki* all the time. They look like strips of tortilla chips covered in powdered sugar, only they don't taste like corn. They're made from flour so they taste like a powdered doughnut with a delicious vanilla pastry crunch instead of cakey dough.

After high school graduation, Amelia, Isaac, and I rented an apartment in Mt. Airy, in the northwest part of Philly. Almost a year later, Selma was born. We were all a little worried she might have to live in the ocean, but she had no outward physical signs of mer-life, like gills or fins. We even tested her skin by sprinkling ocean water on her to see if she had a reaction.

The sad thing was that Amelia's parents never approved of her attachment to "the transfer student." They refused to see her once she graduated from high school. Because of that, they never even knew about Selma. Amelia took that hard, but she adored Isaac and Selma. And she and I were like sisters already. Amelia used to say she had all the family she needed.

We had part-time jobs and took classes at Temple University on a rotating schedule, so Selma always had one of us there to take care of her. Amelia knew how to sew really well, and she worked at Consuelo's Millinery and Tailor Shop. She loved sewing. She could bring home some of the clothes and work on them when she wasn't studying. Sometimes she used her hands, and other times—if she had a big paper due or needed to study for a test —she used magic.

Amelia was studying marine biology, mostly because she loved Isaac, but Isaac wanted to pursue engineering. Having lived underwater, he was fascinated by how things worked on land. He kept his early shift at Mrs. Pulaski's bakery so he could come home between classes, soak in the tub, and take care of Selma. Even though it was unnatural for him to be away from the ocean, he was adjusting pretty well to life on land as long as he could immerse himself daily in the bathtub.

I was an English major with a focus on creative writing, mostly poetry, and my favorite professor took me under her wing and encouraged me to apply for awards, contests, and fellowships. I arranged my courses so that I had almost finished my bachelor's and master's degrees in literature when most students were just getting ready to finish their bachelor's. Because I was studying so hard, I didn't have much time to work, but I found a telemarketing job to help pay for rent, food, and clothes. It wasn't an interesting job, but at least I mostly did fundraising calls instead of selling magazine subscriptions.

Amelia, Isaac, and I had lots of fun joking around and telling stories, even though we weren't together in the same place. Since the three of us were always juggling school, jobs, and Selma, we didn't get to talk and chat like friends sitting on a couch or over meals very often. Instead, we talked to each other in our minds. I would be at work trying to convince someone to give money to save the wildlife species of the week, and Amelia would call me in her mind. She could "see" me from the apartment and tell me a silly joke, like: "What do you get when you cross a bee with a lemur? A beemer!" Meanwhile, I'd be in the middle of telling someone all about the plight of the endangered snow leopard, and I'd just start laughing.

I remember it was the Tuesday of my last week of senior year. When I got home from work, Isaac looked sort of seasick, even though we were on land. We were switching shifts to take care of Selma, but he decided to lie down for a few minutes before work. But before he even made it to the bedroom, he collapsed and hit his head on the hallway table where we kept a bowl of ocean water in honor of his home. The water spilled onto his neck, chest, and shoulders, and suddenly he was gasping for breath. I was holding Selma on my hip and knew there was only one thing to do. I recited a spell to send him home:

> *Oh ocean near*
> *and far away,*
> *to Jersey gulls*
> *and jellyfish,*
> *bring this man*
> *his heart's real wish!*
> *Salamalanunca!*

And then Isaac was gone. I knew he was back in the ocean. And I knew I had to tell Amelia right away before he went too deep. But Amelia had already sensed his call. Just then, I heard her crying in my mind. "Take care of Selma. I'll be back." And then she was gone.

I called—really, I yelled—for Amelia in my mind over and over, but I heard nothing back.

Stunned, I sat on the hallway floor with Selma on my lap. She was two years old. Although I was graduating in ten days and had a fellowship to assistant teach in the English department at Temple, I knew I had to take care of Selma. It wasn't an option to bring her to the ocean since we already knew she wasn't equipped for an underwater life.

I stared at the overturned bowl Isaac had knocked over.

Selma kept asking, "Where's Da? Where's Da?"

"He's on a boat with your mom," I told her. I'm not sure where I came up with that lie. From that day on, whenever Selma asked about her parents, I said they went on a boat trip, there was an accident, and they went missing. I know they're still alive, but that was as close to the truth as I could get.

10

Making Tablas, Meeting Zoraya

Selma

IT'S THE MONDAY AFTER the marathon and I finally finished my chores and all my poems since the Uganda incident. At least that's what Guadey calls our trip. Mr. Finncrisp gave us another city assignment so I picked Granada, Spain, as my next city. I've done lots of research on the Alhambra ever since I bought that postcard in Paris. I even found pictures of the dome of the Hall of the Two Sisters. I love all the mosaics! They're like a colorful puzzle of tiny blue, red, green, and brown tiles that make endless designs on the ceilings and walls.

After school, I find Guadey on the back porch trimming some herbs from her windowsill garden.

"Hi, Guadey! Guess what!" I run up and kiss her on the cheek. She smiles and hugs me with a bunch of spearmint in one hand and basil in the other. The spearmint smell makes me think of chewing gum, and the basil reminds me of Guadey's famous pesto sauce. Even though the basil smells kind of sweet, it makes me think of all that yummy garlic she puts in her sauce.

"I have another city report. I'm picking Granada and I'm going to write about the Alhambra! Isn't that cool?"

Guadey sets down the bunches of herbs on the back porch table. She sits on a stool and puts her hands together like she's praying. After a big inhale and exhale, she says, "Why not Cleveland?"

I drop my backpack on the floor and look at her sideways. "Cleveland?"

"Or, um, Santa Barbara?"

"Guadey, are you serious?"

"Yes, well, not about those places, but isn't there somewhere else in the world you'd like to study?"

"Actually, no. Plus Mr. Finncrisp gave me an 'A' after the chocolate croissants. And I'm going to wow him and the whole class with some *tablas*. I want another 'A.'"

"Okay." Guadey picks up her herbs and heads back into the kitchen. She doesn't look at me.

I pick up my backpack and follow her into the

kitchen. "So Guadey, will you help me make some *tablas*? Please!" I'm trying not to beg, but I'm so excited about building *tablas*, which are basically just cutting boards filled with yummy snacks. It's my favorite way to eat, and the best part is that I know we already have a lot of the ingredients in our kitchen.

Guadey acts funny, her hands are a little shaky, and she's not looking me directly in the eye. But she agrees to help me make some beautiful *tablas*.

We have the perfect cutting board to serve as the base. We start by arranging a few very thin slices of *jamón serrano*—also called "mountain ham"—on the board. It's cured, salty, and chewy. Guadey bought it at the market this week. We add special Spanish Marcona almonds that are a light golden color, and olives. I love olives! Most fifth graders don't, but I love both green and black ones. I only like the ones in olive oil with the pits in them, though.

Guadey always keeps our fridge stocked with my favorite Manchego cheese. It's dry and a little crumbly and also very salty. Guadey slices some bread—a *bolillo*—and puts it on the side. The tabla is so beautiful that I pull my camera from my backpack and take a photo before we eat.

"Guadey, I hope I get to enjoy a real *tabla* piled with delicious goodies in Spain someday!"

Guadey stands as still as a statue looking at me like I just said something scary. "Guadey, are you all right?"

She shakes her head quickly from side to side like she's saying "no," but says, "Yes, yes, I'm fine."

I give her a curious look, but then dig in to my *tabla*. Everything is so good! After we eat, I can't wait any longer to start my research for my city report, especially on the Alhambra.

"Guadey, is it okay if I do some research on your laptop?"

"Yes, honey. I'll peek in on you in a bit."

I leave the table and go into Guadey's study. I power up her laptop and begin searching the Internet.

Here's some of what I find: The Alhambra is a great big castle built by Yusuf I in 1348. It was originally under Muslim control, which means the architecture is full of beautiful, intricate carvings of every kind of shape like squares, circles, octagons, even stars. Plus there's gorgeous Arabic lettering carved into the columns and ceilings. There are even elaborate baths and saunas that used marble and the sun to heat the water. And wow, there are so many neat secret passageways and rooms. I can't wait to go!

Even though Guadey doesn't exactly know we're going, I'm hoping that once she sees how hard I work on my report, she'll take me. I can't believe all the battles and how Charles V took over the city! I also discovered there's a harem area surrounded by the *Patio de los Leones*. The patio is actually this cool circular fountain with lions all around in the middle of a courtyard. Not far from there is the Hall of the Two Sisters, where Zoraya, the sultan's true love and political advisor, stayed. The sultan was the head of the Abencerraje family, and his enemies were always trying to take over. It's rumored that Zoraya's advice kept him in power. After a while, his enemies found out he was getting help from Zoraya and murdered him.

There's a lot more research I need to do, but I already want to go there!

Guadey

It's Tuesday after Selma told me she picked Granada for her city report. She's so frustratingly magical sometimes. It's like her intuition is on overdrive. How could she pick the Alhambra, a place where I have such a volatile history? And she's eating olives all over the apartment and playing flamenco. Then she found my copy of Fairuz Andaloussiyat performing songs by the Rahbani Brothers. She has been playing it so loudly that it's probably audible from the street. The Arabic is jarring lots of memories for me. But what am I supposed to tell her? That she can't pick her favorite city? To quit working so hard on her project because of my past life as a key political advisor to one of the most powerful sultans in Spain's history?

I'm on the back porch hoping this garden can give me some peace. I might as well replant these herbs; I need something to occupy my hands. I spread newspaper on top of our table on the back porch and loosen the basil first. I grab some empty pots and a bag of dirt leaning against the wall. The basil was growing a bit too large for this window box anyway.

Why did I even try to suggest another city? I wonder. *That only makes her want to go to Granada even more.* I can practically read her mind even without "tuning into her channel." I know she's planning a trip. And I know I have to go with her.

I'll have to cast a protection spell to shield us from my past life. I hope this is enough to prevent the spirits from recognizing me:

Zoraya come,
our spirits meet.
Las dos hermanas
be discreet.
Hide from Selma
my past life.
Show only Guadey
free from strife.
Salamalanunca!

There, that should do it.

It's Thursday evening and I know Selma's been working nonstop on her report since she got the assignment on Monday. I'm lounging in the living room on our gloriously comfortable couch while reading Louise Erdrich's *The Beet Queen*. I reread this book every year. She's a poet and novelist so her lyrical lines bring the characters alive for me every time. Uli's asleep on our beige ottoman. I hear the front door unlock and lock again.

Selma runs into the living room, breathless as if she's been training with Hurley on the soccer field again. "Hi, Guadey. Hi, Uli. I have great news!"

I sit up and lean forward. "You do?" *Here it comes.*

Selma opens her backpack and pulls out a stapled pile of papers. "I have a rough draft of my report, and I haven't used magic at all to write it."

"That's great! I know you've been researching a lot."

Selma is rocking back and forth from her toes to her heels with excitement. "I have. And I was hoping that as part of a reward before my presentation and as a celebration of finishing my chores and poems, we could go on a magic-approved trip to Granada."

I couldn't help smiling. "Sure, Selma. We'll go this Saturday."

Selma stops rocking and drops her backpack. "What? Even if I'm not done with my chores?"

"Yes. Even if."

Selma tackles me and locks me in a hug. "Oh, Guadey, thank you so much!"

Uli stares from the ottoman and looks at me like I'm crazy. Even as a cat, he's capable of that look.

"I can't wait to tell Hurley! I'm going to call him right now."

I stand up and catch Selma by the hand before she runs to her room.

"Wait a second. Before you call Hurley, this trip is going to be just the family this time. Maybe I'll take you and Hurley on an adventure this spring."

"Oh, okay, but can I still tell him about it?" she asks, bouncing up and down.

"Sure, that's fine."

She raises her arms palms up to the sky and yells, "Woo hoo!" then runs off to her room.

"I'm going to have to do some important magic before we go," I whisper to Uli, "and I can't risk getting Hurley mixed up in any of this." Uli flicks his tail in agreement. The two of us discuss our strategy in case some old spirits penetrate my protection spell. Then we come up with a transportation spell we can cast from the back porch.

Selma

It's Thursday night and I'm so excited. We're going to the Alhambra in just two days. I called Hurley and he was really surprised Guadey said yes. I am too! I'm going to begin packing today after school. I'll need my *Lonely Planet Guide to Andalucía*, my dark chocolate bar with almonds, my camera, my charger and adapters, and my journal ... plus clothes, of course! Saturday is going to be here before I know it.

Guadey

The Saturday morning of our trip is cold and bright. On the back porch, Selma, Uli, and I each sit on stools around the table. Selma looks at Uli, then over to me with a curious gleam in her eye. "Guadey, is Uli coming with us?"

I smile. "Yes."

"Cool."

"Do you have your traveling satchel?"

"I have my *backpack*, if that's what you mean. And I have everything in it."

I smile at my energetic little girl and reach for her backpack, then lift it up and down to check the weight. "Oh, Selma, what do you have in here?" I decide not to wait for the answer.

"Never mind," I say, "Let's just get going. Uli, please jump up onto the table. Selma, you and I will hold hands across the table and around Uli. He'll sit in the middle of the circle we make with our arms, then I'll recite the spell and transport us together. Got it?"

Uli jumps up and sits on his hind legs facing me. Selma reaches across the table and holds my hands. "Got it!"

Selma cannot keep her body still. If she could run on foot to Spain right now, she'd probably try. She's so fidgety I'm afraid she's going to fall off her stool.

"Ready, Uli?"

"Yes," Uli says with a flick of his tail.

To Granada, take us there.
In circle motion we will be.
Forces strong and present day.
Keep past spirits full at bay.
Bring us sultans, baths, and story
Only in their written glory.
Off we go to Alhambra land.
Keep us together in our stand.
Salamalanunca!

I feel the familiar whirlpool whoosh of magical travel like I've gone down a roller coaster. Then we're standing right in the original courtyard entrance built by Yusuf I. It's a hot day for October, but I remember that was normal when I lived here. And there's that familiar smell of sandy dust and gravel.

"Oh, Guadey, thank you so much!" Selma grabs both of my hands and spins us around in a circle.

"Where's Uli?"

"I'm right here."

Uli is standing in his human form about three feet from us, smiling. He has caramel brown hair, like the fur on his head. His eyes are the same pale Siamese blue. He's wearing dark brown corduroys and a jean jacket. At just over six feet tall, he looks as physically fit as ever. I haven't seen him as a human in a lifetime. I walk over and hug him. It's so good to see him like this.

Selma's mouth hangs open. "Huh? But you're a man."

"Yes, Selma. On this trip, I'm a man," Uli says, his voice deep and playful.

Seeing the palace grounds again and Uli as a human is making me a little teary.

"Cool! I didn't know you could do that. Let's go in! Guadey, are you okay?"

"Yes, just a little woozy from the trip."

"Oh. Well, I'm glad you're okay. Look at the view! Those are the Sierra Nevada mountains, right?"

I nod. Selma reminds me of a pinball. She's darting around us pointing and talking as fast as she can.

"Let's go through the Alcazaba Fortress part first," she says, "and then to the garden and then save the palace for last! Wait! I need to take a picture of the mountains alone and then I need one with you two standing in front of it."

I try to gather myself by breathing in and out slowly. I hope my spell worked to keep my past life-time at bay. There are tourists swarming the area. Their baseball hats, fanny packs, cameras, and phones make them look like they're part of a cult.

As we pose for Selma, I whisper to Uli, "You go ahead to the Palacio Nazares and scope out the spirit realm, then try to find us before we make it to the castle."

Uli whispers back, "Okay. But tell me again why you agreed to come here in the first place."

"Because I knew if I didn't come, Selma would find a way here by herself, or maybe even bring Hurley again. I just couldn't risk it. It's better to be with her than to have to rescue her at the last minute, when someone might recognize me as Zoraya. I couldn't bear it if she was caught in some old conflict."

Uli nods at me and Selma interrupts, "Hey you two, I'm trying to take pictures here! Would you please stop talking and smile for the camera?"

We both turn to face Selma as Uli murmurs out of the corner of his mouth, "I get it."

Selma takes at least five more photos of us smiling, standing with the view of the mountains behind us. "Come on, Guadey, let's take a picture at the fortress! Uli, will you please take a picture of us?" Selma's cheeks are red, her ponytail is coming out of its elastic band, and her bangs are sweaty. She looks as if she just went through a wind tunnel. I love seeing her this happy, but I'm so anxious and alert that the hair on my forearms is sticking up. I really hope the protection spell works.

"I'm coming, Selma."

Uli

I approach the palace quietly, as any lone tourist would. I have no trouble moving around the crowd through the Mexuar—the initial division upon entering the palace. The blue and green geometric patterns on the wall tiles and the carvings of the columns are all so familiar. This is where the Sultan dispensed justice. I walk into the *Patio de los Leones* and the harem area surrounding the patio. I can feel the energy and history of the place with so many battles fought here. I can even sense the days when Napoleon's troops used the palace for barracks. My skin is tingling and I feel a warm tickle up and down my arms and legs. There's a familiar wood-burning smell from my time here with Zoraya. That smell makes me a little nervous because it means there are still some pretty active spirits lurking around these grounds.

I can't quite distinguish all the spirits through my intuitive sight. Visions of thirteenth-century life with Yusuf I and the murdered Abencerrajes family are mixing with eighteenth-century beggars. Selma has no idea, but the head of the noble Abencerrajes fell in love with Guadey and depended upon her smart political insights. She was Zoraya during that lifetime, and I was her friend and bodyguard of sorts. I still went by Ulises.

I suddenly feel a sharp poke under my shoulder blade that's pointy like a spear. "Where's Zoraya?" His voice is rushed and gravelly. I spin around and when I see his face, I realize right away who sent him —Abrahen Zenete. He's the one who murdered the sultan and his family.

"Who?" I ask.

"You know who."

"Hey, I'm just a tourist." I shrug.

He pokes the front of my shoulder now. I wish for my quick cat moves and claws, but I can't change into my cat form in front of all the tourists.

"Come with me," the man growls.

I allow him to push me along toward the maze of aqueducts in the gardens. An elaborate water supply system, they look like pipes sliced open lengthwise running throughout the entire palace grounds. I have to figure a way out of this, and I need to make sure Selma is safe. I glance around for Guadey and Selma but don't see them.

Guadey

"Look, Guadey, we're almost to the palace!" Selma exclaims, taking photo after photo of the architecture, the geometric tiles, and even the sewer covers that say "Granada."

"Selma, don't you want to spend more time in the Generalife Garden? Just look at those fountains." I scan the area, but only see tourists. No sign of Uli.

"Guadey, is there something you're not telling me? You're acting nervous and Uli's been gone for a while."

I realize I'm wringing my hands because my telepathic connection to Uli isn't working. It's probably being jammed by spirits. "No, it's just that I wanted Uli to meet us, and I don't see him anywhere."

I cross my arms at my chest and rub them. Selma

reaches up and gently uncrosses them, puts my hands into a prayer position, and cups her hands around mine. Then she looks directly into my eyes, "We'll find him, Guadey."

I lean down and kiss her forehead. "Thanks honey. Yes, we will."

But I don't know if I believe my own words. I know he's in trouble. I can feel it. The only way I can save him is if I leave Selma for a little while. But what can I tell her? Where can I leave her safely?

"Selma, I'm going to find Uli, but I want you to stay over there at the reflecting pool while I'm gone." It's centrally located and has no roof, which means there are fewer spirits bouncing around and I can sense her better. But I can't tell her that.

She grabs my hand and looks up at me. "Why can't I go with you?"

I wrap my arm around her shoulder and keep us walking toward the reflecting pool. "There might have been a magical snafu. Uli may have turned back into a cat—or something else—so I may have to do some quick spells. I think I can do a better job if I know you're safe and sound." So I tell her a half-truth. Okay, a lie.

"All right, Guadey. I'm kind of scared to be here by myself, though. Something feels funny."

Selma is holding my hand tightly. Her palm is sweaty.

"I understand, Selma, and I want you to feel safe. What if I cast a protective spell around you?"

I feel awful about leaving her and yet I can't risk taking her with me. It might be dangerous.

She slumps her shoulders and looks down at the ground. "Okay, as long as you're sure it will work."

"Look, we're already at the reflecting pool. This was always one of my favorite areas in the palace."

The water reflects the sky's color. It's shifting from blue to a golden glow, signaling dusk.

"What do you mean 'was always a favorite'? I didn't know you had been here before."

I could have smacked myself in the head for misspeaking. I haven't explained my past lives to Selma; although with her imagination, I'm betting she wouldn't have trouble understanding how someone could be one "character" during one time period and then live another life in the future. I point to a pretty marble bench about two feet from the edge of the water. "That's a long story, sweetie. Let's get you settled. I need you to sit on this bench and think about something that makes you feel happy and safe."

"Okay," Selma says, closing her eyes. "I'm going to think about playing marbles with Hurley in our backyard."

I smile and shake my head. My sweet girl goes right back to her best friend. I'm so glad he forgave her. "Okay, honey, I'm going to perform a very special spell that will place you inside of a protective bubble. You'll be able to breathe and see everything, and it will make you feel safe."

Selma squeezes my hand, "Are you sure, Guadey? Positive that I'll be okay here without you?"

I squeeze her hand back, "Absolutely." I smile at her and glance around for tourists. It's nearing closing time and there's no one in this area of the courtyard, so I can do the spell out loud. While doing it silently works just fine, I think Selma will feel better if she hears me say it:

Spirits of a higher realm,
see my child,
her vision pure.
A bubble round,
that is the cure.
She'll feel safe
from now to here
and back again
'til I appear.
Salamalanunca!

Selma

After Guadey's spell, I feel light and full of warmth as though a sun is shining inside of me, starting at my chest. I can see clearly, yet I know I'm in a bubble because I can push out my elbows and they bounce back to my sides.

"Thanks, Guadey. I feel better."

She nods and smiles. "Good, love. I'll be back before it gets dark. Watch the sunset from here. It's beautiful."

The sun is beginning to set and it looks like an orange light has been turned on full blast with the way it's kissing the buildings. This bubble feels like a quilt, so I'm going to curl up on the bench. It looks like it's getting chillier outside now that the sun is going down, but I feel warm and cozy in here. I'm just going to rest my eyes.

The reflecting pool makes a gurgling sound. Then I hear a voice. It sounds so familiar. It reminds me of a song my mom used to sing to me. The tune was so happy, it hopped around my heart. It went something like, "I love you, a bushel and a peck, a bushel and a peck and a hug around the neck, a hug around the neck."

"Selma. Selma, open your eyes."

My eyes are open now. I'm staring at the top half of a woman poking out of the pool. She's wearing a bikini top made of little pearly shells.

"Aren't you cold?" I ask the pretty lady in the fountain.

"No, honey. I'm used to the water."

I stare at her, wondering why she seems so familiar.

"You recognize me, don't you?" she asks with a sweet smile.

"I ... I don't know. Kind of, I guess. But I don't know why."

She glances away for several seconds, breathing deeply in and out. Finally, she turns her eyes back to me. "Selma, it's me, your mom."

My eyes get wide. This can't be. My mom drowned in a boating accident. Or did she? I knew there was something weird about the story. Wait, what is she doing in a fountain? I bolt upright and swing my legs forward so my body is facing her. "Mom? But I thought you were gone."

She pauses. "I am, sort of, but not completely. The thing is ... I live with your dad ... in the sea."

I lean forward. "Huh? Why?"

"Because that's the only place he can live."

"But what about me? Can't I live in the sea with you?"

My mom shakes her head and dips her arms back into the water.

"No, Selma. We're not even sure you can survive underwater, even with magic. I don't want to risk it. For now, we want you to have a normal life with Guadey."

I can't believe what I'm hearing. "Mom, my life isn't normal. I'm inside a bubble, waiting for Guadey to find my cat who turned into a man who might be lost as a cat again."

She bites her lower lip and wrinkles her nose. I think about how I've made that face before. "Well, I guess I mean *a sort of* normal life, with the magic sprinkled in, of course."

I think about that for a moment. Then she says, "I've kept tabs on you. I know this trip was your idea."

"What? You do?"

"Yes."

"So are you saying that the fact that Uli's missing is my fault?" I ask. Suddenly I'm not cozy anymore. My neck, chest, and underarms are starting to sweat. It feels like a big marble is stuck in my throat. Is this a dream? I don't know if I should feel guilty that Uli's lost and Guadey had to find him or excited that I'm actually talking to my mom. I want to ask her so many questions. Why is she here now? Why did she choose my dad over me? But I can't seem to ask them.

She reaches out to me. "No, Selma. I just mean ... oh, I've upset you. I'm so sorry. That's not what I meant to do. I just wanted to make sure you were okay. I was worried when I heard you were coming to the Alhambra."

"But why?"

"Because there's a lot of history here, and Guadey and Uli have had many lives."

"Huh?" My head is starting to hurt from all of this. "Many lives? Does that mean I've had many lives?" I crawl down from the bench and sit at the edge of the pool.

My mom's voice cracks, "I, oh—I'm saying way too much for this first visit." She pushes away from the edge of the reflecting pool and I see a big fishtail flip out behind her. But it's not a fish; it's a part of her body. Wait, my mom is a mermaid? First I thought she was dead and now she's part fish?

"Selma," she says, turning back to me. "Look at the sunset and go back to sleep. Maybe this wasn't such a good idea."

I reach out to her and push against the bubble right as she sinks into the water. "Mom, wait! I miss you! I don't understand!"

I want to cry, but then the bubble starts to vibrate. I try to stand up but it's kind of awkward, because it's stretchy and also a little slippery, so I just stay at the edge of the pool. My mom's gone. I'm crying now—big, snotty, hiccupy crying. Then I notice the sky. It's all those purples, oranges, and yellows of my favorite rainbow push-up popsicle. It's the most beautiful sunset I've ever seen. I inhale deeply so I can start to breathe again without hic-cuping. I climb back up on the bench. Suddenly, I feel so sleepy I can't keep my eyes open.

11

Zenetes vs. Zoraya

Guadey

I START MY SEARCH for Uli around the *Patio de los Leones*. If I come out into the open, I can use myself as bait. Surely, someone from my past is using Uli to get to me. Within a few minutes, I sense two spirits coming from the direction of the baths.

As they come up behind me, I surprise them by turning around to face them. "I know. I'll go with you," I say before they can act. Their shoulders slump down in disappointment. I bet they were ready for a magical fight with Zoraya and never expected me to come willingly.

"Very well," one of the guards says. "We'll need to bind your hands. We don't need your spells botching up our capture."

"We'll get commendations for this one," says the other while wrapping my hands with rope.

"That's fine," I say. Silly, silly boys. I don't need my hands to cast a spell.

They lift me high above the baths and over to the Generalife Gardens on the palace grounds. I'm surprised. I didn't expect to leave the actual palace. It's a good thing it's dusk already because the area is closed off from tourists so no one can see us flying above the grounds. The spirits would be invisible to a normal person, but I'm in the flesh and would be seen.

One guard squeezes my arm tighter and says, "We've got magical barriers coursing through all the aqueducts. So if you try something, you're going to hurt yourself."

I look around at the maze of aqueducts within our area and smirk at him. "I see. You needn't worry."

I'm glad they're transporting me above the gardens. As we float, I have a broad view and scope out the area for Uli. I can come up with an escape plan for both of us once I find him. Finally, we come to a long, rectangular reservoir. I remember this. There are those little crisscrossing fountains that were always so pretty in the morning light. In fact, the exact map of the grounds is coming back to me. The aqueducts are to the right of us, lined with thick bushes. This would be a good place for

Uli to hide if he was able to turn back into a cat.

The three of us land on the veranda at the end of the reservoir. Abrahen Zenete is waiting for me. A short man with squinty eyes, he has that same giant beard. It looks like a family of birds could nest in there.

He's the one who ordered all the Abencerrajes killed—every last knight, every family member, and of course my friend, the sultan. And he blamed it all on me for falling in love. I can't show my anger yet, but my body stiffens as I approach him. I square my shoulders. It's a good thing we're both about the same height so I can look him right in his tiny eyes.

"Ahh, Zoraya." He purses his lips in displeasure.

"I'm Guadalupe now."

"Actually, I'm quite clear that you are Zoraya."

"I was Zoraya, several lives ago."

"This means nothing to me. Why have you come here? Do you want to avenge your love?"

Oh, my goodness! This man has not changed. He's still the misinformed, power-hungry, insecure fool he was centuries ago. I recite a quick spell in my head, loosen the ropes around my hands, and break free. I cross my arms and stand firmly on both feet. "I'm vacationing."

"And you brought Ulises, your most fervent ally." Zenete hisses as he says Uli's name.

I think about how I've got to find a way to get a message to Uli so he can check on Selma as I say, "Who are you talking about, Abrahen?"

"Ulises the Magnificent."

I put both hands on my waist and step closer to him until I'm standing just two feet away. His guards start toward me, but he waves them off.

"I'm sorry, but I don't know who you're talking about." If Uli is listening, he's going to get a kick out of this. He hasn't been called Ulises the Magnificent for centuries.

"Don't play games, Zoraya, or I will kill him."

"How do I know whether to be upset by your threats to kill Ulises if I can't even see him? Your guards must have stowed him somewhere."

I lift my arm in an arc, ready to slap him across the face. I'm poised to lunge at him and push him to the ground when he leans back and shields his face with his arm. His guards try to grab me, but I fling my arms up, turn around, and stare them down. Then I turn back to face Abrahen.

"You have poked and prodded me, then brought me to your feet. You slaughtered an entire family, not because the sultan loved me, but because you knew I was the source of the most savvy political advice of the time." I clench my fists. "This many hundreds of years later, can I not come back to this country that you stained with your jealousy and rage?"

I step even closer so we're only a foot apart.

My anger causes the water of the reservoir to bubble. Steam rises and it looks like a giant pot of boiling water. The crisscrossed fountains shoot streams like fire hoses on full blast. I shout at him, "Now you want to kill more?"

Zenete pushes himself farther back in his chair. He's grimacing and turns his head sideways like he's bracing himself for a slap or worse.

Uli

I'm being held in a small rose garden about two hundred feet from Guadey. I can hear her shouts and the sounds of the nearby fountains bubbling over. The two guards next to me look nervous. I think they know it's time to leave or be subjected to Zoraya's wrath. I pretend to struggle so they can at least act like they tried to prevent my escape before running away.

Once they're gone, I head straight to the clump

of bushes, crouch down, and transform back into a cat. It's so nice to have my feline moves again, especially my ability to prowl silently, unnoticed. I can see Guadey now.

"Well, do you? Do you want to kill more?" Guadey shouts at Zenete. Her hair rises in a semicircle like a half moon above her head. Her nostrils flare. Oh man, she's about to do a big spell. She puts her arms at her sides with her palms facing him. In a forward scooping motion, she lifts her arms and chants her spell:

> *Zenetes full of pride, deceit*
> *Spilled blood of knights and children too.*
> *Know my wrath, Zoraya's power,*
> *Abencerrajes' vengeance our desire,*
> *Come knight, come sultan in ire's way,*
> *Show Zenete he must pay!*
> *Salamalanunca!*

I've never seen Guadey this angry. I hope the spell doesn't go overboard and awaken more spirits, or even topple the palace buildings. I hear footsteps now, lots of loud, pounding footsteps. The spirits of the knights of Abencerraje with the sultan in tow, barrel around the corner toward the courtyard where Guadey and Abrahen are facing off. The fountain is bubbling like a cauldron on high heat. The sultan is dressed as elegantly as ever in deep green silks. His tunic seems to float behind him as he approaches. Guadey always talked about his green eyes, but I didn't remember how bright they were. The knights, though, they're a vision of death. They're injured, bloodied, growling, and looking for the Zenetes. These revenge stories, especially in the spirit world, can last forever.

Like Guadey, I've had multiple lifetimes and have seen the same kinds of battles fought again and again. The minute they see Guadey or "Zoraya," they're going to blame her for their downfall as well. She was the brains behind the sultan's politics, and in their simple deduction, her relationship with the sultan instigated their last battle and final demise.

The knights make it around the fountain and head straight for Guadey and Abrahen. Five knights rush Zenete and yank him by his limbs. The remaining knights stand and glare at Guadey.

The sultan shouts, "Zoraya! Run! They blame you! Run. Please, I beg you. You survived once. You must again! Please!"

It's time for me to do some magic. I slink out of the bushes, crouch down, and get ready to leap right over the fountains. Whoa! I lose my footing right before leaping when two figures suddenly rise out of the bubbling fountains. I haven't even done my spell yet!

Water shoots straight up in the air. Holy smokes! On top of the waterspout in the middle of the fountain is Selma's mom and dad, Amelia and Isaac. They're glowing and majestic. They're so breathtaking that everyone stops fighting to stare at them.

Amelia is shimmery in a gold and green bodice. Little shells seem to move in circles all over her body. Her tail is made up of tiny octagonal scales that alternate gold and green. Isaac's tail glistens blue and silver. Arms straight out, he grips a thick silver rod with a set of white feather wings on either end. Amelia springs up in an arc and catches the middle of the rod while Isaac holds it on either side of Amelia's hands. They look at each other and hum a haunting and hypnotic tune. I'm stunned motionless by the beauty of the melody. Then they start to sing:

> Alas, Alas,
> Wings of Peace,
> Feel them washing over me,
> Help these knights to sleep.
> Help these knights to sleep.

Alas, Alas,
Wings of Peace,
Feel your light shine on me,
Let these spirits find some rest,
Lift the stains from their baths,
Lift their souls into one.

Alas, Alas,
Wings of Peace,
Feel them washing over me.
Feel them washing over me.

Holding the rod, Selma's parents spin so fast that all I can see is a circular blur of blue and silver, green and gold. I feel like I'm being hypnotized by their melody. One by one, the knights and Zenetes lie down. As they surrender to sleep, their bodies become translucent and shimmer away.

Guadey's eyes are closing. She looks sleepy too. But when the singing stops, she's wide awake again. The fountains drop to their normal height, and Selma's parents flop back down into the pool, with their torsos above the water line.

In my cat form, I rush over. So does Guadey. Amelia and Isaac meet us at the corner of the fountain.

Guadey looks at her best friend and starts to sob. "I couldn't control it, Amelia."

"It's okay, Guadey," Amelia says, reaching out to her.

But Guadey is kneeling at the edge of the fountain, with her elbows on the ledge and her head in her hands.

"No, it's not. What if Selma were here?" Guadey says.

Amelia gently pulls Guadey's hands away from her head and squeezes them between her own until Guadey finally looks up.

"She's fine," Amelia says.

"How do you know?"

"Because I visited her."

Guadey yanks her hands away from Amelia and shakes her head no from side to side.

"I know, Guadey," Amelia says, "but she was getting scared, and I just missed her so much."

"But what are we going to do? What do I tell her when she says she saw you here?"

Amelia grabs Guadey's hands again. "She'll remember it as a dream."

"A dream ... but I don't know if I can count on that. You haven't been around to witness her smarts, her curiosity, or her magical power as she's grown. I bet she's going to figure out that it wasn't a dream." Guadey shakes her head again. "I also feel terrible about lying to her. She deserves to know the truth soon."

I walk over to the bushes, transform into my human state, and come back to interrupt them. "It's getting dark. We better go get Selma."

Guadey hugs Amelia. Isaac and I share a half hug, half handshake. I walk over to Amelia, and she reaches up and squeezes my hand.

Then Selma's parents turn away from us. Both hold the magic rod as if they're on a trapeze, elevate, swing up and over it once, then drop down into the fountain where they disappear, the rod vanishing with them.

When we return to find Selma, she's asleep and smiling on the bench inside her bubble. It's quiet in the courtyard. With no one around, Guadey uses magic to transport all of us to the hotel.

Guadey

After all the excitement and drama, we sleep soundly at the Hotel Anacapri. In the morning, I'm the first awake and dressed—and I look the worst because I'm worn out. I place a glass of fresh-squeezed orange juice and a pitcher of water next to

Selma's bed. The sounds wake her, and she opens her eyes with a yawn. Before I can even say "good morning," there's a knock at the door. It's Uli. His sandy brown hair is sticking up a little.

Selma laughs at him. Uli smirks. I swear if he had a tail, he'd flick it at her. "Go ahead, say it."

"Bedhead! Bedhead! You have bedhead!" Selma laughs.

"And what do you think you have?" Uli asks with a smile.

Selma peers at herself in the vanity mirror above the dresser. Her bangs are sticking straight up in the air, and she has a big hair lump on the top of her head. She can't stop laughing. It's contagious. I finally laugh too.

She bounces out of bed and gives me a morning hug. "You look tired, Guadey. How about if we just hang out in Granada today and eat?"

It's such a relief to hear her say this that my shoulders drop and I can actually feel the tension from yesterday leaving my body. It seems as if she has no memory of seeing her mother.

"That sounds perfect. We'll have a light breakfast, and then we'll have *tablas* or *tapas* later."

"Great!" Selma says as she bounces off to the bathroom to get ready for the day.

Thirty minutes later, we leave the room for the lobby restaurant and order *cruasanes de mantequilla* —like mini buttery croissants—and cups of *café con leche*. Selma licks her fingers in delight with the *cruasanes*. Then we head out of the lobby to wander the streets. We walk until we hit a small plaza I remember well.

When we arrive at the plaza, the vendors are already out selling tiles with letters and numbers on them. I let Selma pick 1441 for our address and spell out "Calderón." Selma picks white tiles with bluish-purple numbers and letters wrapped in yellow vines. Seeing Selma and Amelia's last name spelled out in tiles after visiting with Amelia yesterday, even under those dangerous circumstances, just makes me miss her more.

Two men across the cobblestones from each other are selling the exact same bullfighting posters. They rubber-stamp tourists' names on the posters with black ink. Selma's excited about that, but I don't think she'll go for it because of the disturbing picture of the bull being stabbed with an *espada*, a kind of sword.

"I really want a picture of a flamenco dancer," Selma says. "Hey, there's a small poster with a man and woman dancing! Guadey! Look, flamenco!"

My coffee's kicking in and I'm feeling better. "You know, Selma. I think that would look nice in your bedroom."

"Really?" She turns to face me with her hands clasped together in front of her chest.

"Really."

"Wow, this is so much fun. Thanks a lot, Guadey."

I reach over and stroke her hair. "You're welcome."

Uli taps me on the shoulder. "Hey, Guadey, didn't you say you wanted some spices while you were here?"

"I did." We meander over to a woman with two long rows of burlap sacks filled with spices. The colors are so rich—deep reds, electric yellows, vibrant greens, and earthy browns.

"Oh, Guadey. Are we going to cook with these?" Selma leans over the spices and inhales.

"Something like that." I smile at the woman behind the sacks.

She smiles at me. Uli and I know her as Pemba. She was selling spices in the same spot back when I was Zoraya and Uli was a palace guard.

Pemba nods at Uli with a gentle, blushing smile. Uli nods and says, "You're looking lovely and colorful, the same as always, Pemba."

Pemba's smile widens as she looks at me. "What now, Miss Zoraya? What brings you back for some of my wares?"

"Ahhh, Pemba, it's Guadey now."

I stretch across the table to kiss her on both cheeks and inhale a blend of cardamom and ginger. Pemba always smelled like a fresh cup of hot chai. It feels good to connect with my old friend.

"Pemba, this is Selma."

Pemba reaches across the table and closes both of her hands around Selma's. She whispers, "Selma, I see the water in your eyes."

I look at Uli and send him a mental message to change the subject.

"Water? Like tears? I'm not crying," Selma says.

Thank goodness Uli heard me. He palms Selma's head playfully. "No, Selma, we know you're not crying," he says. "So, Pemba, tell us what you have today."

Pemba folds her hands on her belly. "Cloves. I have cloves fresh from Zanzibar. Little stars to help you wish for anything in the world."

Selma jumps up and down. "Oh Guadey, can we get some little stars?"

I have to take a deep breath now because Selma is going to take lots of mental notes, and I don't want her to learn too much, even from Pemba's passing comments about the spices and their magical powers. Food magic takes an entirely different level of skill. Dabbling and experimenting can lead to misdirected love, anger, even death. I want to take advantage of this trip—and I need lots of Pemba's wares to restore my supplies back home—but Selma is such a sponge for information. I'm going to have to keep the spices locked away.

"Yes, Selma, I plan on getting quite a bit." I nod at Selma and point my chin at Pemba. "Okay, friend, please take us on a spice tour."

"My pleasure!" Pemba says. "First, I have bay leaves, which are nice for sauces, stews, and other recipes. If you place them in a cloth bag and crush them, they'll triple in potency. Be careful not to eat them, though—they're just for flavor." Pemba winks at Selma.

Oh dear, this is only going to increase her curiosity. I run my palm from my forehead down my nose and cover my mouth.

"I wish I didn't leave my notebook in the hotel," Selma says.

"It's all right, Selma," I tell her. "There's plenty of time to learn. Just take in the colors and smells. You'll remember what you need to remember."

Selma takes my advice literally and leans over

Pemba's larger bags of spices that are lined up along the side of her table. "I smell cayenne, yellow curry, ground cloves, and cinnamon. Those last two smell like you, Guadey! I love them!"

I hope Selma doesn't remember too much just yet. She's been hard enough to keep up with lately. Pemba turns around and busies herself with a wooden box big enough to fit four pairs of shoes. She bangs on the top and on the right side. I watch Selma try to decipher what Pemba's doing, but it's hard see around her ample hips and her rainbow of layered skirts. That's a good thing.

Pemba turns back and hands me three bottles filled with thin rusty red filaments. "Here you are, Guadey. Saffron—three stigmas to one flower. Each bottle has two ounces. That's a full day's work!"

Selma is on her tippy toes trying to sniff the bottles. "So how do they get the—what's it called? Stigma? Out of the flower?"

Pemba rests her hands on her belly. "One person handpicks them individually, then dries and roasts them until they're this lovely rust color."

Selma makes an imaginary telescope out of her hands and peers into the bottles. "I'd say that's roasted, rusted, red! Hey, that sounds like a poem in the making!"

Uli and I inhale sharply. Pemba smiles at us. What Selma doesn't know is that those three words are part of a powerful saffron spell one can perform prior to adding them to a food dish. Depending on the strength of its spellmaker, it has the power to control the eater's actions for a certain period of time.

"Great, Pemba," I say. "So we'll take the cloves, bay leaves, saffron, curry, coriander, nutmeg, and a lot of rosemary. I'm going to bake some into bread."

"What about *hiliki*?" Pemba says as she taps a bottle.

"Man, I wish I brought that notebook!" Selma says. "What's *hiliki*?" She's so excited right now that she's dancing a twist back and forth.

"It's Kiswahili for cardamom," I say. "And yes, Pemba, we'll take some green and white."

"Lovely! Here you go, Zor—I mean Guadey."

"*Asante sana.*"

"What's *asante sana*?" Selma asks, bouncing from foot to foot.

My friend does the honor of answering Selma's question this time. Pemba bows slightly forward, "It's 'thanks a lot' in Kiswahili."

Selma opens her mouth to ask another question, but I interrupt her before she can speak. "It's a long story, Selma. Let's just say Pemba has roots in East Africa—Zanzibar in particular."

I nod my thanks to Pemba as we walk away.

"East Africa!" Selma says, skipping. "Wow! I could have asked her about Zanzibar. You know I want to go there too, Guadey, right?"

I look at Uli for a little help and thankfully he interjects. "Selma, you need to focus on enjoying the present moment. Remember, you're in Spain now."

"Oh yeah, you're right, Uli. So, Guadey, why didn't we have to pay Pemba?"

"Oh, Selma, you ask so many questions. Let's just say that Pemba owes me. We have a history, so she gives the spices to me as gifts."

"Magical gifts?"

"Yes, Selma, magical gifts."

Selma's eyebrows lift and she giggles. "Wow! That's so cool!"

I grab Selma's hand and loop my other arm through Uli's. "Yes, Selma, it certainly is."

The rest of the day is perfect. We walk toward the cathedral until we reach *Calle Oficios*. I smile when I see our destination and say, "we're here."

Selma reads the sign out loud, "Bar Sevilla. Why did you pick this place, Guadey?"

I step behind her and hold both of her shoulders. "Take a good look. One of the greatest writers in Spain's history used to come here regularly."

Before Selma can ask who, Uli jumps in. "It's Federico García Lorca. Among other things, he's famous for writing about *duende*."

Selma spins around. "*Duende*? What's that mean?"

I take her hand and lead her inside. "I'll explain later. But for now I can tell you it's kind of like that feeling when you get a spell just right." Selma looks up at me and grins. I think she gets it. Once we grab a table, I lean back and take in the black-and-white photos on the walls. I tug on Selma's sleeve. "See that photo? That's Carmen Amaya, the most famous flamenco star in history. Legend has it she began dancing in a cave right here in Granada. She learned when she was only five years old."

Selma's eyes grow wide, "Wow! I have to learn more about her!"

The waiter approaches and brings us a complimentary *tapa* of thick Spanish *tortilla*, which is similar to an omelet mostly comprised of onions and potatoes. The *tapas* include rolled pieces of *jamón serrano* and Marcona almonds, like we make at home. But these almonds are toasted and cooked with salt, cayenne pepper, and butter. We also eat olives, marinated goat cheese, and Manchego cheese. Then we order one of Selma's favorite dishes in the world: dates wrapped in bacon. The dates arrive perfectly caramelized, sweet and salty at the same time. The waiters also bring us olives with tiny pickles and anchovies on a toothpick—not Selma's favorite. I'm sure her city report will be filled with lots of food and spices.

I have a nice glass of *rioja*, a local regional wine found only in Spain, and Uli tries the *sangría*, which is a wine punch made with fresh oranges, lemons, peaches, and other fruit soaked in the wine. Selma leans toward Uli's glass and looks at the fruit floating inside. She declares, "I'm going to make sangría with grape juice instead of wine as part of my report." She's having fun sipping her *agua con gas* (which she calls "bubble water") with lemons floating in it. After we eat, we sit for a long while watching the tourists and Spaniards go by.

By the time we return to the hotel room in the evening, our bags are packed with a little spell I did while at the restaurant. Uli walks into our bathroom and closes the door. Soon after, he emerges as a cat. Selma's no longer surprised by Uli's ability to do this. "Hi, Uli," she says, as if she's seen him transform her whole life.

It's time for me to get us home.

Pemba's wares
and little stars
Spirits here,
Spirits now
bring us home,
show us how.
A girl, a woman, and a cat,
take us slowly where we sat.
Salamalanunca!

12

Home Again

Selma

On Monday I see Hurley in the hallway next to our lockers. "Hi, Hurley! I've missed you!"

"Me too, Selma. Where were you this weekend?"

"Spain! Guadey and Uli took me."

"Wow! I'm so glad you had permission."

"I know. It was funny, though ... Guadey was a little weird about going."

"Really?"

"Yeah, but then she seemed okay once we were there."

Hurley nodded.

"I'll show you my pictures. I'm going to download them in Mrs. Cushing's computer lab. She has a cool photo bookmaking program I can use to make an album from our trip. I can write captions and create neat designs. You want to come?"

"I can't right now. I have to go to Mr. Finncrisp's room to make up a test."

"Oh, okay then. I'll meet you in the cafeteria at lunch."

When I get to Mrs. Cushing's class, I go straight to my favorite computer in the corner of the room. The computer is already turned on, so I insert my memory card and watch my photos appear one by one. There are some really funny ones with Uli and Guadey talking—their expressions look super silly. I can't stop giggling as all the beautiful colors pop up in picture after picture.

Suddenly, X walks into the classroom. He's always sweating—his face, his underarms—there are stains on every t-shirt he owns.

"Hey, Selma, whatcha doin'?"

My whole back gets tense when I hear his voice. "Working on my city report."

He's walking closer. I see him looking at my pictures. "You know, Selma. I think your city report should become my city report."

I stand up and turn around, holding my chair in front of me like a shield. "Mrs. Cushing said she's coming right back."

He glances toward the door, then walks over to me. "You don't mind if I grab your camera do you?"

Now his face is real close to mine and his breath smells like spicy chorizo sausage. The greasy smell hits my sinuses, making me nauseous, scared, and angry all at the same time. This is definitely a moment to use magic at school. I'm finally going to do a vision-blurring spell—and I don't feel bad at all because he asked for it. I'm glad I've been practicing my mental spells so I don't have to say it out loud. I start reciting it silently:

> *Call blurry eyes*
> *And spirits' surprise*
> *Stay back and away*
> *Bad breath at bay*
> *Lose him in a fuzzy haze*
> *Shield me from this bully's gaze*
> *Cucalacas!*

He's not reacting. Did I do the spell wrong? Why isn't my magic working? X leans closer and reaches for my camera with one hand and shoves my shoulder with his other. I stagger backwards and lose my grip on the chair. "Give that back!" At least he hasn't stolen my memory card with the pictures. I want to cry and scream at the same time. I'm wishing for the bubble from Spain. For Guadey. For my mom.

Mrs. Cushing enters the room. I'm still gripping the chair in front of me and crying.

"Selma, what's the matter? Xavier, what's going on?"

"Oh," he says, "Hello, Mrs. Cushing." He shoves my camera in his pocket.

"What brings you to my classroom, Xavier?"

"Oh, Selma needed help on her report. Isn't that right, Selma?"

"No! That's not right! He has my camera in his pocket." Tears are streaming down my face. There's a knot in my throat and it's getting dryer and dryer and bigger and bigger. I glare at him, wondering what happened to my magic. When Mrs. Cushing's cell phone rings, X tries to skip out. Mrs. Cushing blocks the door, which is hard because X is bigger than she is. It's Guadey on the phone, and she asks to speak to me.

"I know what happened, honey," she says.

"My, um, you know, wouldn't work."

"That's my fault, Selma. I'm so sorry ... I'll be there right away."

I feel sick inside and hand the phone back to Mrs. Cushing. They speak for a moment, then hang up. Mrs. Cushing looks puzzled, probably because of the timing of Guadey's call, but she hugs me as we wait for Guadey.

Guadey arrives in less than five minutes. She holds me until I stop crying and can breathe normally again. Then she looks at X and says, "What did you do to her?"

"Nothing, I just found her camera and was about to give it back to her." He pulls the camera from his pocket and holds it up.

I yell, "You're a liar! And a bully!"

X shrugs and tries to laugh it off but his eyes are darting back and forth between Guadey and me. I know she's giving him one of her stares. "Come on, Selma. You know I was just playing around."

"You pushed me."

"No, I didn't."

"You're lying again!"

Mrs. Cushing puts her hand out and says, "The camera. Now."

"Here." He hands the camera to Mrs. Cushing who hands it to me. X tries to play it off, but I know he's scared of Guadey.

The four of us head out of the classroom and down the hall to Principal Catania's office.

Mrs. Catania stands up at her desk when we walk in. Mrs. Cushing speaks up first. "I walked in on an incident between Xavier and Selma in my classroom."

Mrs. Catania narrows her eyes and looks directly at X. "What happened?"

Mrs. Cushing says, "When I walked in, Xavier was standing very close to her. Something definitely happened right before I arrived."

I take a deep breath and wipe my nose with my arm. "X tried to steal my camera and my city report. And he shoved me!"

Mrs. Catania takes a deep breath and turns to X. "What do you have to say about this?"

"I was just fooling around. Selma doesn't know how to take a joke."

Guadey places her hands on my shoulders. She says, "Look at Selma. Xavier has been bullying her and Hurley since the beginning of the year. But she's being brave in speaking up."

Mrs. Catania nods at Guadey and says, "It's clear to me that we need to set up a proper meeting between all of us and your father, Xavier. I'll be calling him at the shop."

X backs himself against the wall. "No, please don't call him. Can't my older sister come?"

"No, Xavier. We have Selma's guardian here. Your sister is not your guardian."

"But then he'll have to close the shop. He'll lose money. He's gonna be so mad."

I've never seen X look so scared. I almost feel sorry for him. Almost, but not quite. Mrs. Catania looks at me. "I wish there were something more I could do. For now, I can promise to set up a meeting with Mr. Serrano."

"That's a start, Mrs. Catania," Guadey says, "but it's not enough."

Mrs. Cushing hugs me and says, "You let me know if you need anything during the day at school, Selma. Anytime. Okay, honey?"

I nod. I can't talk or else I'll start crying all over again. Guadey takes my hand and we head toward home. She's tearing up as she says, "Selma, I'm so sorry. After your trips to France and Uganda, I decided to freeze your magic at school for your own safety, just for the time being. I feel terrible now for not talking to you about it first."

I'm confused and exhausted as Guadey tells me how she set a magical alarm to alert her if I was in danger or tried to use magic. She tells me about how she used magic to appear at school, but had to do it carefully by transporting herself to the bathroom at the Blue Kangaroo Laundromat next door so no one would see her.

When we get home, I rush into my room, flop on my bed, and hug my pillow.

Minutes later, Guadey brings me a cup of hot chocolate. "Selma," she says, smoothing my hair, "I'm going to make sure you always have a protection spell on you and that you can use your magic at school again."

"Okay, Guadey," I say. "Thanks." I'm still angry at Guadey and X. And I'm scared to go back to school. I just want to crawl under my covers and feel safe again.

~

Guadey

When I get back to the kitchen, Uli is waiting for me on the chair by the fridge. I'm so furious, I can feel my halo of hair rising like it did in Spain.

"Uli, I don't know what I'm going to do about that boy. Where should I begin? I want him to feel as afraid as Selma did. I want him to stay away from her forever."

Uli talks to me sternly in my mind. "Guadey."

I bend down and put my face close to his nose. "What?"

He licks my nose with that sandpaper tongue. "Stop."

"What?" I wipe off his smelly cat saliva.

He's now talking a little less loudly, but still firmly. "Stop. Breathe."

"But there must be consequences! He's been harassing Selma and Hurley from day one. And it's my fault she couldn't use her magic." I keep having flashes of our recent near battle with the Zenetes. I know I'm starting to cross over into dangerous territory again.

"Guadey, you must be creative with your consequences. You must breathe."

I take a deep breath. "Fine, you're right. I have to learn from Granada." I pace the kitchen. "Wait, remember the itching spell I used once when we lived in Puerto Rico?"

"Oh yes, on one of your unwelcome suitors. That seems like too much on a boy."

I'm already composing the spell in my head. "I've got it, Uli. I can tone it down a bit. I'm ready to cast it now."

"Not too intense, Guadey."

"Don't be silly, Uli. This will just be a mild itch for a little while, and it will only occur when he gets close to Selma. I'm going to include Hurley in the spell for his own protection."

I stand up and take three deep breaths. Then I slowly raise my arms with my fingers spread apart.

Fleas and ticks
prickly heat
itching arms
that can't be beat!
X Serrano shall not reach
for Selma, Hurley
this shall teach.
Itching round him day and night
preventing now
my sweet child's fright!
Salamalanunca!

After reciting the spell I feel a little better. I go to Selma's door and knock. "Can I come in?"

"I guess."

Selma sits up in her bed and pulls the covers up to her neck.

"Honey, how are you doing?"

"I'm—I'm kind of mad at you."

My stomach twists. "You should be. I shouldn't have frozen your powers. The alarm I set went off, but I didn't make it there in time." I kneel at her bedside and touch her foot poking up under the blanket. "What did he do?"

"He wanted to steal my city report, which made no sense, and then he took my camera and pushed me. I thought he was going to punch me next."

My ears are getting hot. My hair rises again, but I know I have to remain calm for Selma. Selma's eyes get a little wide when she sees my hair rising around my face like I'm charged with electricity.

"What he did was wrong, Selma. And you should be safe always, especially at school."

"Why does he always pick on me and Hurley?"

"Well, honey, I don't know that much about him, but did you see his face when Mrs. Catania said she was calling his dad for a meeting? He looked scared. Scared like he made you scared. It almost made me wonder if his dad is sort of a bully too."

"Maybe ... but all I know is that I'm not going back to school."

"Well, sweetie, Xavier won't be giving you problems for a while. Let's just say he'll be itching to get away from you."

I reach out to soothe Selma by stroking her hair. She shrinks away at first, and then she leans into my hand. We hug and I crawl into bed beside her. I really want to use magic to erase her memory, but that could cause her serious confusion in the future. I have to help her work through her feelings of fear and anger. It makes my heart tight and achy to think she feels betrayed by me.

I snuggle with her and sing her a beautiful song. There's no spell, just pure love flowing from my heart.

My little Selma girl,
your heart is full and sweet.
I wish you so much love
from your pigtails
to your feet.
You are my shining light
in afternoon and night,
and always in the morn'
we give thanks
that you were born.
My little Selma girl,
your heart is full and sweet.
You teach us to believe
in everyone we meet.
Our family is quite strong,
a circle so complete.
Sleep now my darling child,
and know
our love cannot be beat.

Selma

The next morning, I'm awake before Guadey. I'm not as mad at her as yesterday, but I still don't want to go to school.

I think about dreaming of my mom in Spain. I'm going to try to conjure her in my dreams again. I play with a spell in my head:

> *Where there's water*
> *you are loved,*
> *also from the sky above.*
> *Your daughter waits*
> *in questions true,*
> *asking history of you.*
> *Crossing into sand time now,*
> *my eyes close shut*
> *showing how.*
> *Mom, I need you when I sleep,*
> *you have promises to keep.*
> *Cucalacas!*

That just might work, but I'm going to save it for later. I wonder if when I recite it in my head like that it might help my mom reappear sooner. Right now I just want some waffles. Guadey ended up sleeping in my bed last night. She's still asleep with her back to me, kind of squishing me against the wall. I nudge her. "Guadey."

She turns over on her back. Her hair is a beautiful brown crisscross mess all over her face. She mumbles, "Yes, Selma."

"I don't feel good. I don't think I can go to school today."

Guadey turns on her side to face me. We're snuggled together almost nose to nose under the covers.

"What if I told you X won't bother you for sure today? Would that help?"

"Yes, but how do you know?"

"Let's just say I know."

I squint my eyes in disbelief.

"Tell you what, I'll restore your powers at school with a silent spell right now."

Guadey lies on her back again and smooths the hair away from her face. She closes her eyes and gets quiet. I wish I could hear the spell, but at the same time I don't want to. It would just remind me that she never told me she took away my magic in the first place. When she's finished, Guadey opens her eyes, turns back on her side to face me, and smiles.

I ask her, "Can we go to White Palace Grill for waffles before school?"

"Sure. Hurry up and get ready, and I'll use magic to get us there."

When we walk into the restaurant, the white tiles are just as shiny as ever and it smells like bacon, eggs, and pancakes. Elena, our favorite waitress, takes our order. I sit and stare out the window.

After a bit, Guadey asks me, "Selma, honey, what are you thinking about?"

"My mom."

"Oh."

"I want to dream about her again."

"Dream about her?"

"Yeah. In Spain I dreamt that I found her in the reflecting pool where you left me in the bubble."

"Selma," Guadey says, reaching over to touch my hand, "you can dream about your mom all you want."

"But it was so real."

"That's how dreams can be."

Elena brings us the waffles. I put my face down over the waffle and inhale the steamy vanilla malt aroma. It's such a delicious smell, it actually makes me happy before I even take the first bite. I think of

Hurley and pray a silent thank you prayer like when he says grace. Then, I slice the waffles and pop the first airy piece into my mouth. I don't even need much syrup. "Oh, Guadey, these are my favorite! Thank you for bringing me here today."

"You're welcome."

Guadey orders pancakes and one egg over easy. She keeps the three pancakes stacked and slices them into triangles. Then she breaks the yolk of her egg so that it spreads on the pancakes. She takes her fork and dips one triangle into the yolk, then she lifts it to her mouth and chews. The happiest smile spreads across her face.

Once we're done, Guadey pays at the register and leaves a generous tip for Elena. She takes me to the bathroom, which luckily is just one room, so no one else is in there with us. She recites the spell to take us to school:

> *Take us now from Waffleland*
> *To swimming clothes and dryer sheets.*
> *We shall appear from bricks behind,*
> *May no one see or pay us mind!*
> *Salamalanunca!*

We pop right out of the bricks behind the Blue Kangaroo Laundromat, and Guadey turns to walk toward school. I grab her sleeve to stop her. Standing firm, I cross my arms and tell her, "I still don't want to go to school."

"I understand, Selma. But sometimes it's good to get these kinds of things over with quickly. He won't bother you. I promise. Remember, you have your powers back at school just in case."

My throat gets tight. My face is heating up. I look down at the ground and say, "Okay."

Mrs. Catania is at her usual spot at the front door of school to welcome students. When she sees me and Guadey, she smiles, then leans down and tells me, "I'm keeping an eye out today, Selma. Please don't hesitate to come see me if anything else occurs."

My body relaxes. "Thanks."

Guadey kisses me on the cheek, strokes my hair, and heads back down 18th Street.

Guadey

I walk home slowly because I need time to think. I approach Oxalá, a *botánica* and gift shop. The sign outside Oxalá says *El Sol Sale Para Todos*—the sun comes out for everyone. I go in to see if I can find any inspiration for my next move with Selma, Amelia, and Isaac. Maybe I can set up a meeting with them at the lake. I'm afraid, though, that when Selma finds out the truth about her parents, the hurt will compound the trauma she just suffered at school. But I realize now that it's time for the truth to come out.

"*Hola*, Guadey," Oscar the owner says. He's sitting behind his desk in the far corner of the store. We're the only two people there.

"Hi, Oscar. How are things?"

His gift shop is filled with natural oils like sandalwood and bergamot, homemade candles and soaps, artwork on silks and canvas, plants, cards, and jewelry from artists throughout Chicago. I can lose myself for hours in here.

"Better than for you."

"Oscar," I say, "I know you can read energy, but do you have to be so obvious about it?" At his desk, I pick up a piece of clear quartz then set it down again.

"Well, you seem very confused and all twisted up in a knot. In pain."

"Oh, Oscar, I'm trying to decide if I should tell the truth about something."

Oscar nods. I pace the perimeter of the store like

a caged lion. I keep talking without looking at him. "It's just that the truth could really hurt someone I love."

He nods again.

"And she ... well, I already made a big mistake just yesterday and caused her a lot of pain because I didn't tell her the truth about freezing her ... oh never mind." I can't believe I almost talked about magic out loud. "I guess I know what I have to do. No wonder she's always bending the rules. Look at me!"

Oscar offers me a calm smile without showing his teeth.

"Oscar, thank you so much. I feel more clarity now."

"Good. Can I interest you in some lavender soap and rose water? That will help you stay clear-headed and relaxed."

I smile and buy a double batch.

Selma

Before I get to homeroom, Hurley runs up to me in the hallway.

"Selma! Where'd you go yesterday? I thought we were going to meet in the cafeteria. I waited for you but you never showed up." Hurley's hands are on his hips waiting for my answer.

I look down. "I had to leave."

He touches my shoulder. "What happened? Was it a magic thing?"

I take off my backpack and twist the straps in my hands. "No, it was at school. It was X." I can feel the lump in my throat coming back.

"Yeah, I hear he got suspended."

I lean toward Hurley and whisper, "When I went to Mrs. Cushing's class to make my photo book from the Spain trip, he pushed me and tried to steal my camera. He wanted to take my report. It was scary."

Hurley balls his hands into fists at his sides. He opens and closes them again and again. Then he takes a deep breath and hugs me.

"I'm so sorry, Selma. He better not come back around here." He lets go and asks, "So did you try to use your magic to defend yourself?"

"I tried my blurry vision spell, but my magic didn't work."

"Why not?"

"'Cause Guadey froze it."

"Aw, man, Selma. I'm so sorry." He frowns and shakes his head.

"Yeah, me too. Mrs. Catania is going to talk to his dad. He's pretty freaked out about that."

"I bet. Come on, Selma. Let's get to homeroom."

I lean my head onto his shoulder and he loops his arm in mine as we walk into the classroom.

Later that week, Hurley and I walk together to Mr. Aguirre's music class. Hurley's being extra sweet and wraps his arm around my shoulder as we stroll down the hallway. I haven't seen X all week because he was suspended for three days, and he's supposed to be back today. Mr. Aguirre is playing an upbeat song as we find our desks and sit down. Once everyone is seated, he says, "'When Johnny Comes Marching Home Again' is an oldie but a goodie written by Patrick S. Gilmore. You guys need to feel the beat." X rolls his eyes and groans. I notice he has a black eye and his cheek is swollen. I can't help but wonder if his dad did that.

Mr. Aguirre pounds out the beat with his hands on a small drum he holds under his arm. He sings, "When Johnny comes marching home again. Hurrah! Hurrah! We'll give him a hearty welcome then. Hurrah! Hurrah!" He sets the drum down and walks around the room singing and handing out one piece of dark red construction paper to each student. A few kids are banging on their desks to the beat.

Everyone's looking at him, waiting, but he just keeps singing. Finally, after all the papers are passed out, Mr. Aguirre says, "My dad was a funny guy. He liked to dance and sing, and he used to play records every day when he came home from work. The whole family would dance—even my mom while she made dinner. My dad loved the Spinners. The Stylistics. The Moody Blues. Then one day he got called to war. It was the Vietnam War—they called it a conflict, but it was a war. Everybody, it seemed, was against it. Anyway, my dad went away, and I never saw him again. For a long time I didn't listen to music, and then I realized I had to celebrate the time he was here, so I started playing his records. His name was—" He leans down and writes something on his piece of construction paper. Then Mr. Aguirre tapes the paper to the wall. He pats the paper gently and says in a loud happy voice, "His name was Valente Aguirre."

He turns to us. "We're going to make a wall of remembrance by building it brick by brick. Anyone who has lost someone, I invite you to write his or her name or initials on the brick. Even if that person just went away and hasn't come back and you miss them, please honor them on your papers by writing their name or initials."

I know I can write my parents' names, but since X is in the room, I just use initials. The last thing I need is for X to make fun of me for my dead parents. So I write A.C. & I.C. for Amelia and Isaac Calderón. Even though Calderón comes from my mom's side, I always think of my dad as Calderón too. Hurley writes W.B. for his dad. And X actually writes the name of his brother, Rodolfo Serrano. When I was in the cafeteria during the first week of school, I heard X's friends talking about Rodolfo. He was a soldier in Afghanistan and came back pretty changed. He was nervous a lot and didn't leave the house much except at night. The rumor is he had such bad nightmares, he couldn't sleep. Then one night, he left the house and never came back.

Hurley and I tape our bricks next to each other. It seems like every kid in the room has a brick to put up. The only one with a blank brick is Clare O'Connor. She's just sitting there with her green eyes wide open and her paper on top of her notebook. Then I see her slip the paper into her backpack. Hurley interrupts my spy work. "What are you doing after school? Do you want to come over?"

"Yeah, definitely."

"Cool."

I can't wait to go to Hurley's. I actually just want some normal time with him losing at marbles.

13

Plates

Selma

THE REST OF THE school day is pretty uneventful. I send Guadey a text asking permission to go to Hurley's after school and she texts back "yes" right away. I keep thinking about Mr. Aguirre's class and my parents and then about Clare. How can she not have lost anyone? I think she's a bit of a mystery. She has that Celtic knot ring from her grandmother in Ireland. And she tried to move in on my friendship with Hurley, but she's just so nice. I can't be angry with her about it.

When I walk by Mrs. Cushing's classroom, I suck in my breath, trying to focus on my after-school plans with Hurley instead of remembering what happened there.

I've never been to Hurley's house because his

mom usually works late, and she doesn't like him to have friends over without an adult home. But his mom has today off for a "mental health day." Hurley explains it to me as we leave school. "Basically, she takes a sick day every once in a while. She says it's to recharge her batteries."

We walk across the street from school to the other side of Harrison Park toward Laflin Street. On the way to his house, Hurley tells me, "I still find her on the computer just like she's at work, but she's doing her own digital art and graphic design."

Hurley's house is the third one in a row of four connected houses. We walk up four steps to get to his front door. He pulls his keys from his backpack and unlocks it, saying, "After you, my friend!"

I look all around Hurley's living room. About a dozen plates, the size for salads, hang on the walls exactly level with my eyes. *Why would she hang salad plates on the wall?* I wonder.

"Hurley, what's up with those plates?"

"Oh, my mom has had them forever."

"Really? What are they for?"

"They all have a meaning, but I can never keep them straight."

"I can tell you what the salad plates mean," Hurley's mom says, coming out of the kitchen. *I didn't say salad plates out loud*, I think. *Wait, did she just read my mind?* Her hair is cut short and close to her head, and she wears a floor-length, dark purple dress that shows off her waist. The dress makes me feel like I'm in the middle of a public television special—one of those shows where people have British accents.

"Hi, Mrs. Bingenworth."

"Hello, Selma."

"Thank you for letting me come over today."

"I'm glad you're here." She glances up at the wall. "Would you like to know the meaning of the plates?"

"Yes, please!" I'm rocking back and forth, front to back, with a bounce.

"Let's go around the room starting over here." She walks me to one side of the turquoise sofa and begins explaining the plates one by one. "This first one, with the diamond figure eight in the middle, is for riches. And this next one," she says pointing to one with a sun within a moon, "is for fertility."

"Do you want to have a baby?" I ask, wanting to trace my finger on the sun.

"No, Selma," she says with a chuckle. "There are actually several areas of life that can be fertile—work, wealth, and spirit, for example."

I nod as she points to the next one. "Now this next one is 'against the sorrows of mortality.'"

"What does that mean?"

"Well, it's sort of like a good luck charm after something bad has happened. You know how bad things sometimes happen to good people? Well, this helps them with the sad feelings." I make a special note of this drawing. It has an eye inside of a triangle, and the triangle is inside of the sun.

"Gosh, Mrs. Bingenworth," I say, "this is so ... magical. I thought you were really religious."

"Yes, Selma," she says, bending down to my level. "I'm full of faith in God and in many positive wonderful powers. Religion holds its own magic. Faith holds another. They can overlap. And there is much more. I believe in a world of possibilities."

I love the way Hurley's mom knows so much and is willing to share it. Not like Guadey who will only teach me little bits at a time.

"Wow. Will you tell me about the other plates?"

"Perhaps during another visit," she says, standing up. "Right now, why don't you and Hurley go have a snack? There's a special treat for you two in the kitchen."

Hurley leads me into the kitchen where the walls are bright yellow, almost glowing, and the curtains are the color of bright green grass. There's a tower of hot chocolate chip pancakes piled on the center of the kitchen table. They are shielded with a glass cake cover with a handle.

"My favorite!" Hurley says. "Thanks, Mom!"

Hurley pulls plates, forks, and napkins for us, and Mrs. Bingenworth puts the bottle of syrup on the table and removes the glass dome.

"How many do you want, Selma?" Hurley asks.

"I'll have two, thanks."

Hurley piles three pancakes on my plate and slides the pile of chocolate deliciousness over to me. "Trust me, you're going to want three."

I smile. "I trust you."

Hurley serves himself four pancakes and says his grace. "Thank you God for my friend Selma and may these chocolate chip pancakes soothe her soul. And also, may she play marbles with me for the rest of my life. Amen."

I giggle and then say, "Amen." I'm so lucky to have Hurley.

We both dig in. Wow, the chocolate chips are hot but not too melted. The pancakes are so fluffy and light. I can see why Hurley thinks I can eat three.

"Yum! This is an awesome snack! Your mom is an amazing cook!"

Hurley answers me with a mouth full of pancakes. "I know! She is, isn't she?"

After eating, we play marbles. Today he uses up the last hole punch on the frequent marble champ card. It's the one in the center with the triple game. I'm glad we've hole-punched the entire card, but I'll keep playing marbles as long as he wants to play.

While Hurley takes a bathroom break, I wander back into the living room and look at the symbols drawn on the plates. Mrs. Bingenworth comes in, carrying a small purple bag tied with a blue and purple striped shoelace.

"Selma, I want to give you a gift." She hands me the bag. "Carry this bag with you, and keep it to yourself."

"Wow, thank you so much, Mrs. Bingenworth. What's inside?"

"Three talismans. I made them out of rocks from the Eno River in North Carolina. One is 'Against all sorrow.' Another is 'To win healing from the sun,' and the last is 'For relief from pain.'"

A lump forms in my throat again. "How did you know I needed these?"

"That's the thing with faith and magic, Selma. There's a way of knowing. You'll get to that point. Someday, you'll probably even teach others. You just have to be patient. Don't underestimate patience. There's a path and a journey for you. Try not to jump ahead on that path. You may not be ready for what you learn."

"Okay. I can't promise anything, but I'll keep patience in mind."

Mrs. Bingenworth puts her hand on my shoulder, leans down, and looks me in the eyes. "Selma, remember, you have a journey. Try to be patient while you're on it."

I smile at Mrs. Bingenworth and give her a long hug. She wraps me up in the folds of her purple dress. I feel so safe here.

14

Soleymani

Guadey

I WAS ACTUALLY RELIEVED WHEN Selma asked to go to Hurley's after school; it's nice to have some mental and physical space to myself. I crawl into bed and fall into a deep, deep sleep, and when I wake up, I smell the wet roots of mangrove trees and taste the sea on my lips. Soleymani!

We used to meet in the thicket of mangroves when we were just twenty and twenty-one years old. He always joked that I was the older woman. I remember noticing him on the first day of our Caribbean Poetry class. While reading Derek Walcott's *Omeros*, I looked up from my book and saw him gazing at me from the second row. I was in the back row, hoping the professor wouldn't notice that I was skipping ahead to read more poetry instead of paying attention to his lecture.

Soleymani smiled. His black Chicago White Sox cap was turned backwards. (Who knew I'd end up in Chicago? Maybe Soleymani did.) I knew he was different somehow, that he wasn't a regular mortal, but I had no idea of the depth of his power.

Suddenly, it felt as if our surroundings moved in slow motion. Things were blurry except for Soleymani. I had a fleeting thought that he had put a spell on me. But I swatted the thought away like a fly.

Then, I felt water, and the two of us were sitting by the shore with our toes in La Parguera Bay. Soleymani transported us from the classroom to the mangroves. I could see an endless maze of roots through the clear water. He turned to me with a big smile full of straight, white teeth. His skin was chestnut, with beads of sweat carpeting his angular nose. I smiled back and said, "I knew it."

"What?" He gave me a half smile with his bright teeth hidden.

"That you had powers."

"Oh, yeah?"

"Yep. You act like you're this regular old Temple University student, but your light is too bright."

He dropped his head on my shoulder and said, "Yours too."

I pushed him away playfully and said, "So, what are we going to do?"

He stood up, waded into the water and said, "How about a swim?"

And that was our first mangrove meeting.

I also remember our last trip to the bay. He whispered to me, "You go first." And so I did. I swam and swam underwater, then blew bubbles while thinking a spell:

Bahía, bahía,
hear my call!
Cerebellum, bubble,
lights and flicker,
phosphorescent
water thicker.
Hail the day inside the night,
show me,
show me
Yemaya's light!
Salamalanunca!

I found myself far away from the mangrove trees and surrounded by tiny greenish-yellow lights made by the phosphorescent "lightning bugs" in the water. I marveled at the way the sea danced. Even the coral seemed nimble. Then Soleymani came up behind me and put his arms around my waist in the kind of love hug that made me know safety and sureness. When I turned around to face him, his black hair was long, wet, and flat against his egg-shaped head. His smile was so big and bright that his eyes were almost closed.

"You took a while to catch up and find me this time," I said. I liked to tease him that my powers were stronger.

"No, I just wanted to watch you wonder at the magic, the glowing, and the water. You always light up just like the *fosforescentes*."

"I still can't believe we can do spells without talking."

"You just did, love. When you thought it, you recited it, and you conjured a new reality."

I need to get out of bed, but first I stretch and do a quiet mental spell in Soleymani's honor:

> *Oh gingko now*
> *so full of light,*
> *yellow dancing,*
> *spinning flight.*

Your sis has fallen,
brother too!
Ancient leaves,
show what to do.
Salamalanunca!

The mailman outside clicks open the set of four metal mailboxes. It's time to get up and think about making dinner. Mr. B. is walking on the other side of the street and waves. I wave back and open our mailbox. I pull out three envelopes and a newspaper circular. One envelope is from the Orcas Island Writers Festival, confirming that I'm teaching a workshop. I had almost forgotten I agreed to teach there before we even moved to Chicago. The festival takes place during the week of Halloween. This is just what we need. I think Selma can use some time away. She has always wanted to go to the San Juan Islands—it's on her "list." I'm going to make it a surprise.

15

Doe Bay

Selma

ALL HALLOWS' EVE IS less than two weeks away, and Guadey likes to make a big deal of it. This year she's taking me out of school for a whole week so we can go on a trip to a surprise place. She tells me to pack warm clothes, a bathing suit, a flashlight, a camera, and my journal.

School doesn't make me nervous anymore because Guadey's spell made sure X is staying away from me for a long time, hopefully forever. He starts to scratch his arms whenever he gets close to me. Plus, I have my powers back at school. I even went into Mrs. Cushing's class, and we worked together to create an awesome photo book from my trip to Spain.

Since the weekend I visited Hurley's house, I've spent more time reading my library books. After seeing those plates and having the talismans Mrs.

Bingenworth gave me, I've wanted to learn more about the power of symbols with the spells. I'm still wondering about Hurley's mom. Hurley's always joked with me that his mom stresses all her rules, and I've just taken it to mean she's super strict and would never be open to our magic way of life. Boy, was I wrong.

I found a rock in Harrison Park on the way home from school last week. I picked some symbols from the library books and used a permanent marker to draw an eye, flames, and a snake on it. So now it's a talisman against falsehood and deception. Then I added it to the bag Hurley's mom gave me.

Finally, Halloween week has arrived! We leave today, October 27. As the sun rises, Guadey and Uli are waiting on the back porch with Guadey's wooden spell box. I have my suitcase, talismans, books, dark chocolate bars, and journal.

"Ready, Selma?"

"Yep!"

"Uli, are you ready?"

Uli flicks his tail.

"Selma, I'm going to do this spell by myself and bring both of you with me. Is there anything you want to tell me before I do this spell? It's a complicated one."

"Um, I have some talismans with me."

Guadey lets out a big breath. "Let me see them. Who gave them to you?"

"Hurley's mom. She gave me three and I, um, made one."

When Guadey sees the one I made, she almost drops my purple bag.

"Selma, we're going to have to set up a bit of a magic study plan for you. This self-study you're doing can be perilous."

"Hurley's mom sort of said the same thing. Something about not rushing my journey. Why does it matter if I learn magic a little faster than you teach me?"

"I'll explain it to you, but not now. We have to get going." Guadey takes a deep breath.

Running round
through space and time,
this sacred week we will find
sweet harmony and muse's gifts.
Healing waves and sun's strong ray,
please take us now
to Doe Bay!
Salamalanunca!

We all appear with our bags behind a swing set on a hill. Ahead of us, I see a gathering of small cabins and the most beautiful blue water. There's a gray building down by the water and a white sign with black writing that says, "Doe Bay General Store."

I start crying, I'm so happy. "Guadey, is this Orcas Island?"

"Yes, Selma, it is. We're staying here at Doe Bay."

"Oh Guadey! It's beautiful! It's magical! It's—" I drop my bags and run toward the water. "Look at the evergreen trees and those giant rocks! They have a general store! That's so cool!" I've moved from crying to laughing. I'm so happy. I have to jump around little piles of deer poop as I run. I turn to face Guadey and Uli and yell with my arms up in the air, "Well, it's called Doe Bay for a reason!"

That evening Guadey hosts a reception and open mic night to launch the writers' festival. Uli stays behind in the house, which is named "Doe Baby." He opted to remain a cat and enjoyed sleeping in the bay window all day. He's awake when we leave with our flashlights to walk across the grass to the café.

I'm so excited. The café is filled with silk wall

hangings from Nepal covering beautiful walnut-colored wood. We sit in a booth and the waitress brings us a menu. Everything is made from Doe Bay's organic garden. She comes back with two glasses of water and asks for our order.

"Guadey, is it okay if I order for both of us?"

"Sure, Selma."

I turn to the waitress. "May we please have the squash blossom pizza with arugula pesto, pine nuts, and squash, and two iced teas?"

"Sounds great!" the waitress says, smiling as she heads to the kitchen with our order.

While we're waiting for the food to arrive, the event organizer introduces Guadey and invites her to share a poem. I love watching Guadey perform her poetry. I like to think about her as a superhero. She's sort of a "super poet." All her magic seems to glow and float in the air with each line of her poems. As she approaches the microphone, I swear the audience can feel her light. Tonight Guadey reads a new poem dedicated to Soleymani. She sways a little back and forth before starting and then begins reciting:

Skies for Soleymani

Skies open in cerulean
Can I swim to you?
My braids twist
in a map of mangrove roots
tangled up by flashing neon
Will I taste fresh water tonight?
Feel you tracing my mind's eye
down my nose
to gentle embrace?
Conjure my heart above the sand
bring it down from cumulus dreams
visit middle lakes
and me
palms open
waiting

I'm curious about Soleymani and wonder who he is. I never think about Guadey falling in love. He has to be an old boyfriend. I wonder why she never mentions him.

After the reading, lots of writers approach Guadey to congratulate her. She walks back to our table and sits down just as our pizza arrives. It's so beautiful that it looks like a painting. The tiny yellow pine nuts are set off by the bright green pesto. And the squash blossoms look like bursts of orange sunshine. Guadey serves us each a slice. I bite down and savor all the flavors in my mouth: garlic, basil, and a thin, crunchy crust. I can't believe I'm actually eating a flower!

"Guadey, this is the best pizza I've ever had in my entire life! What do you think?"

Guadey smirks, takes a bite, then grins. "You know, Selma, I think it's the best pizza of my life too."

After dinner, we stroll back to our cabin. Uli jumps up on the couch next to Guadey. She saved him a bite of her pizza, and he flicks his tail as he eats it, then licks his front paw and cleans his face. I wonder if Uli minds having to lick himself clean all the time as I head toward the bathroom to take a shower with the diluted Dr. Bronner's Magic Soap they supply at Doe Bay. Everything is so natural here. I love it.

The week is filled with a lot of fun. It's pretty cool outside, enough to wear a sweater and a jacket, but I don't mind. The air feels fresh. It's like a cleaning system for my nose and lungs. The sky feels open, not like in Chicago where I can almost always see the tall buildings of the skyline like a fence guarding the city. Life here feels slow, simple, and peaceful, so different from the noise of the "L" and the smell of the buses and cars. Guadey has time during the day to take me to Cascade Lake, where she casts a heating spell in the water so we can go swimming. We're the only ones in the water because no one swims here in October.

Afterward, we go hiking in Moran State Park. Guadey borrows the Doe Bay resort van so we can drive all the way to Mt. Constitution. From the summit we can see snow-topped Mt. Baker over on the mainland. There's so much beauty everywhere we look. In East Sound, the main town, we find lovely shops filled with ice cream, crafts, and clothes. There's even a consignment store where after hours, when it's closed, people can still pick something off the $3 rack outside the store and slip the money in an envelope through the mail slot. There's so much trust here. Chicago feels like another lifetime. The only person missing is Hurley. I'm taking detailed notes in my journal so I won't forget anything to share with him.

It's five in the morning on October 31. I'm waiting on the rocks above the water. It's still dark as night, and I've wrapped myself in a green flannel blanket, sipping black tea from a thermos. I clutch my bag of four talismans as I make out the little dipper. I'm waiting anxiously for the first oranges and purples of the morning. The man at the general store told me that at dawn, seals might come out to these rocks.

I sit very still, even though my fingers itch for a pen and a lantern to write by. I wish that my camera, with its giant flash, was big enough to capture the stars. My sweatshirt hood covers my ears, so when I hear the first big nasal blow, I wonder if it's just the waves. But when I hear slapping against the rocks, I know the seals are nearby. I close my eyes and think about the legend of the silkies, those seal maidens who wandered too far onto land and became human. *Will I see a seal girl come up over the rock?* I wonder. *Could I become a seal girl?*

I push my hood back from my ears to hear better. I feel peaceful and still. Under normal circumstances, I'd conjure a spell to give me "super" hearing. But this time, with my eyes closed, I can almost see the seals, they sound so close. When I open my eyes, I see two people in the water below. I blink hard, wondering if I conjured something without meaning to.

When they don't go away, I squint to see them better. Then my eyes get wide. It's like my dream in

Spain. I realize I'm seeing my mom, and this must be my dad. I'm so confused. How could this be? Is this a magical trick? I clutch my purple bag of talismans and slowly climb down to the water's edge. My mother has black hair and blue eyes. My dad has dirty-blond hair with streaks of green, like seaweed. His eyes are brown like mine.

"Selma." They both say my name at the same time.

I press the fingers of one hand into my eyes and say, "I'm dreaming."

They both lean on top of the rocks with their arms outstretched to hug me. My mom says, "No, dear, we're here. Really here."

I back away from them. "You? You can't be! You're not! You're not! Why are you saying this to me? This is a mean joke. You're dead. Drowned. And now you're here all wet. This isn't funny at all."

My dad says, "Selma, it's true. We *are* here ... and we love you so much."

I turn around and look at the house where we're staying. Guadey is running toward me. The next thing I know, she's hugging me from behind. I push her arms away from me, but I'm so shaken up that I end up leaning back into her.

"Guadey, this can't be," I say.

Guadey's voice is shaky. "I know, I know. It is, though. It is."

My chest tightens. It's hard to breathe. My nose is tickling.

"Why now?" My eyes are filling up with tears and then I start to sob. I'm crying and sad and angry all at the same time. How could they have lied to me? Why did they leave me?

Guadey turns me around, bends down, and whispers, "It's that fourth talisman you made, the one against falsehood and deception. It made this possible. It's my fault for not telling you the truth sooner."

~⌒〇

Hildegarde, Hurley's Mom

Back in Chicago, I wake with a start. I brew my Assam tea as I do every morning and say my prayers quickly over the altars, laying my hands over the teacup to read the leaves. A snake appears, then breaks into a fork—a fork in the road. I know Selma has sped up her journey. I close my eyes and utter the blessings on the back of the three talismans in her bag.

Sorrow be dust and dust dissolve
Let all my grief go into this grave.
My orb and rays
Grant thee ease.
Who meets my eye
Her pain must fly.

~

Selma

All of a sudden, I feel my purple bag get warm. I turn back around and stare at my wet parents. "I know you chose each other over me," I say. "And Guadey, you, and Mom and Dad—it even feels weird calling you that—you all lied to me! Every day since you 'went on a boat'—it's all been one big, giant lie." I use my sleeve to wipe my tears. I can feel my words jumbling around in my stomach, making me want to throw up. I push Guadey away, then walk back down to both of my parents. "Why now? Why are you here? This is my dream trip, and you've ruined it!" I stand there with my arms crossed. Suddenly I start shaking and feel extra cold.

Guadey's crying too. She rushes down after me. "Selma, this is what Mrs. Bingenworth referred to when she talked about rushing your journey."

I turn around. "So you're saying this is all my fault?"

Guadey comes closer, grabs my shoulders gently, and turns my body to face her. She leans forward with tears streaming down her cheeks. "No, it's our fault—the adults' fault. We didn't tell you the truth because we didn't want you to hurt this way, to feel 'not chosen.' I wanted to build my life around you. So did Uli. And we did just that. It's been my greatest joy."

I hadn't noticed, but Uli has been walking in figure eights through my legs and purring.

I look at Guadey's tears and fall into her embrace. "I want to go home," I sob. "Guadey, I want to go home now."

"I know, honey. But how about you, Uli, and I go back to the house for a while to talk. We can't run away from the truth anymore. Your talisman made sure of that. Our journey is what it is."

"Selma," my mom says from the water's edge. I turn to look at her. It's weird to hear her call my name and it's also familiar. She reaches up with one hand. "Please know that I'm sorry. I know you're upset, but I was so young when I left to follow your dad."

I want to stay mad, but I also want to hug her. I look at my parents closely, seeing glimpses in the half-light of their fish tails swaying underwater. I say to my mom, "So that really was you in Spain? I didn't dream it?"

"Yes, it was me. I shouldn't have appeared then, but I just missed you so much."

"So are you going away again? Are you disappearing forever?"

"No, Selma. I'm always with you. Anywhere you're near water, I can get to you. That's why Guadey, your dad, and I chose Chicago. My life now is in the water, but I can visit with you ... if you want me to."

"Me too," my dad says. "It's my fault, Selma. It's these fins. I tried to live on land. I really did. But now that we've reunited and you know how to find us, I really want to get to know you."

I crouch down and grab one of my mom's hands and one of my dad's. "I want to know you too. But why can't I go with you?"

"You're just not made to live in the water, sweetheart, at least not now," my mom says.

I kick the sand and ask, "So how long can you stay?"

"Not long," my dad says with sadness in his voice. "In fact, we have to leave now."

"Why?" I ask, wanting to cry again. "Why do you have to go so soon? You just got here."

"This was an unplanned visit," my mom says.

"Your magic called us. But we'll see you again, I promise. From now on, though, I need you to listen to Guadey and to Mrs. Bingenworth. You do have a lot to learn, my girl. It's dangerous to dabble."

"Wait," I say, "how do you know Hurley's mom?"

"We can see things, Selma. That's all you need to know right now."

I pause for a moment, then take a deep breath, exhale, and stand up. I look down and see two stones on the shoreline—one flat, smooth, and oval, and one shaped like a round, rough ball. I pick them up and hold them to my heart. Then I give the flat one to my mother and the round one to my father.

"Take these and feel me always with you."

"Oh, Selma. We always feel you. Always," my mom says. "But these will help us touch you too."

My parents say, "We love you" at the same time. It feels like a song, one I've been missing my whole life.

I lean down and hug my mom and dad and they both hold me. Even though they're wet, it feels so good. Then Guadey puts her arms around me. "They'll be back before you know it," she whispers.

"I know," I say. "Now I really do know."

The rims of Guadey's eyes are red. "I can't believe I'm going to say this, but we have to get going. I have to teach a workshop this morning."

My dad waves at Uli. "Later, Uli. Thanks for looking out for my little girl." Then he looks at Guadey. "And thank *you* ... for everything."

"It's my pleasure. She's my joy."

I look over at Guadey and smile. My stomach has calmed down now.

My mom waves at Guadey, "Thank you, my dear friend. I'm sorry for all the confusion and pain I've caused. I love you and know someday we'll find a way to be together."

They both call out, "Goodbye honey. We love you."

"Goodbye, Dad. Goodbye, Mom," I say as my parents sink quietly into the water, their heads disappearing into the choppy morning waves.

I turn around and look at Guadey. "You're sure they're going to be okay? That they can breathe and won't drown?"

"I'm sure," she says. "Are *you* going to be okay?"

I reach up and grab Guadey's hand. "I think so."

Guadey, Uli, and I walk away from the water and up to our cabin. Just before we go into the house, I stop and turn to Guadey. "I'm going to have a lot to tell Hurley. And you're going to owe me some serious payback of my favorite meals when we're back in Chicago. *And* I want to know about this Soleymani guy."

Guadey stops walking, nods, and kisses the top of my head.

I look up at her. "And, if you want me to tell the truth, you have to tell the truth too."

Guadey smiles and pulls me into a tight hug. "Done."

Dear Reader and Magical Spellmaker,

Thank you for choosing to spend time eating, traveling, and discovering with Selma, Hurley, and me! If you want to stay in touch, here's how to find me:

www.rebeccavillarreal.com
Check out our Tribe & Family Book Club Guide and more!

Email:
rebecca@rebeccavillarreal.com

Facebook: www.facebook.com/
Rebecca.Villarreal.Writer

Twitter: @RebeccaVWriter

Instagram: rebeccavillarrealwriter

Pinterest: www.pinterest.com/RebeccaVWriter/

Remember to tag your posts: #cucalacas

I love mail too!

Rebecca Villarreal
1072 Casitas Pass Road, #180
Carpinteria, CA 93013

There is a second book in the works, so if you enjoyed *The Amazing Adventures of Selma Calderón*, I hope you'll stay in touch.

Want to help spread the joy of Selma and Hurley? Please take action and:

1. Write a review on Amazon.com.
2. Lend your copy to a friend or better yet, buy a copy for someone!
3. Ask your local library to order some copies.
4. Share your photos via social media with #cucalacas.

Together, we'll build an online community to inspire, educate, entertain and, of course, cook up a storm!

Sending you love and magic,

Rebecca

PS: You'll be glad to know that 5% of net profits from this book are donated to organizations that benefit youth.

Acknowledgments

This book is a love letter to you, dear reader. My heart opens every time you meet Selma, Hurley, Guadey and so many more. Thank you for spending your precious time with us.

After dedicating more than a decade to this story, I must thank three people first. My husband, José and my son, Jacob: you have been my dream come true, helping me make *this dream* come true. Victor Hodge has been my most faithful reader from the very first chapter to the last. You made me believe this day would come and it would be BIG. (Yes, you're allowed to cry now.) To my blood family, Mom, Joe, Mike, and Natta, to the Gilberts and the Kazmierczaks—thank you for always cheering me on. To my tribe for your protective circle: Terry Edwards, Amheric Hall, Courtney Hedderman, Michelle Corrigan Ríos, Kristen Arps, Cecilia Mandrile, Morocco B. Assouline, Judie Urba, Heather Heppner, Tindi Selma Amadi, Estela Astacio, Karen Cushing, Lhatoya Reed, Dara Dann, Megan Crowley, Regina and Greg Baiocchi, and Father Jerry Boland. To my RBBP Nurture Huddle & Cohort Circle for the gentle push to leap, especially Lindy Stockton, Katherine Carey, Katrina Davy, Sheila Pai, Maria Rodriguez, Vanessa Sage, Jan Blount, Jacqui Crocetta,

Michael Nelson, Kiala Givehand, Pascale Recher, Kelly Pfeiffer, Jennifer Vanderbeek, and Melanie Grimm. Monica García, you came into my life in a big way when I most needed you as a friend, a guide, and an *hermana*—thank you from the soul center of Bekita Linda.

For the building of a dream, you need a team of people to help you with design, blueprints, construction and sanity hugs (virtual and live). For their generosity and talent, I'll always be grateful to: Susan Crowley, Glenn Gemmell, Peg Giglitto, Colin Ryan, The Arroyo Family and the Lakeshore Homeschoolers. Gracias to my early family readers who bolstered my courage: The Hoch Family, The Menkart Esparza family, and Susana Cárdenas.

To my book birthing team: Beth Barany (as my doula creating the space to encourage gentle growth); Stacey Aaronson of The Book Doctor Is In (as my doula coaching me to push and breathe, using her heart, mind, pen, and artistry to help me elevate Selma to her safe space); Alvaro Villanueva of Bookish Designs (for "getting" me and Selma and creating a cover that's as beautiful as it is edible); and Erika Friday for holding my hand through labor now and for helping me manifest world peace through fun, fiction, food, and family for years to come.

Thank you Eléazar Delgado of Café Jumping Bean and Kelly Lynch of Scafuri Bakery for feeding and caffeinating me on either end of this creative process. Special appreciation goes to the CTA Blue Island #60 bus drivers for providing me with a mobile writing studio.

I'm forever grateful for an awesome job working with inspiring retired educators and school personnel who teach me to love and treasure life every single day.

I also have some folks who've imparted specific skills to produce a work like this and to show up with courage and vulnerability. Special admiration and spirit Namaste to: Thich Nhat Hanh, Julia Alvarez, Louise Erdrich, Jennifer Lee & the Right-Brainers in Business, Marie Forleo & the B-School Community, Danielle LaPorte & The Desire Mappers, Mayi Carles & the Life Is Messy Kitchen Community, Chris Guillebeau, Brené Brown, Elizabeth Gilbert, Iyanla Vanzant, and Oprah Winfrey.

There are more, so if your name isn't on paper and you've helped me, consider it written in my heart's memory.

And to God, *La Virgencita de Guadalupe*, Buddha, the Faeries, and my Angel Guides, I'm humbled by your gifts and I promise to keep noticing.

Links for Amazing Adventures

I've placed some links below to help you begin exploring some of the topics covered in *The Amazing Adventures of Selma Calderón*. Keep up the curiosity, find more links on your own, and share them with your tribe!

Great Books and Resources:

http://www.teachingforchange.org
http://weneeddiversebooks.org
http://www.rethinkingschools.org

Recipes & Our World's Food

http://www.lifeismessykitchen.com
http://www.chopchopmag.org
http://www.immaculatebaking.com/goodies/recipes/
http://foodbabe.com
http://robynobrien.com
http://kriscarr.com

Staying Active

http://www.letsmove.gov
http://www.girlsontherun.org
http://www.blackgirlsrun.com

Writing, Self-Esteem & Courage

http://www.amightygirl.com

http://www.writegirl.org

http://kidpresident.com

http://www.sarahselecky.com

http://brenebrown.com

Travel & Wildlife

http://www.visitphilly.com

http://www.choosechicago.com

http://www.lonelyplanet.com/france/paris

http://www.alhambradegranada.org/en/info/
   historicalintroduction.asp

http://www.ugandawildlife.org/explore-our-parks/

http://www.awf.org/

http://orcasislandchamber.com

https://doebay.com

Bullying & Child Abuse

http://www.stopbullying.gov

http://stopcyberbullying.org

https://www.childhelp.org

About the Author

Author Photo: Tim Arroyo

REBECCA VILLARREAL has climbed with mountain gorillas in Uganda, listened to seals snort on Orcas Island, felt the spirits at the Alhambra in Spain, and eaten countless baked goods in Paris. She's a big believer in the magic of everyday life. Featured in *The Washington Post* and the *Chicago Tribune*, a seasoned writer and artist, Rebecca has been published in multiple literary outlets for more than twenty years. Please join our family at:

www.rebeccavillarreal.com

Your spells, notes, and recipes go here!